Bruce's rumina‾‾‾‾‾‾‾‾‾‾‾‾‾‾‾‾‾
clack sound of ‾‾‾‾‾‾ moving at high speed,
borne to him through the stillness of the night.
As he discerned the faint pin-pricks of light from
the first carriages of the Royal Mail, Bruce shone
his torch onto his watch. It was exactly 3.02 am.
The train was on time. It was a good sign. Bruce
picked up his walkie-talkie. His voice was deliberately, almost exaggeratedly, calm, betraying
no trace of the mounting excitement and nerves
leading almost to nausea that he knew he and the
rest of his men were feeling.

'It's coming down, chaps. This is it.'

BUSTER

*A novel based on his own original
screenplay*

Colin Shindler

SPHERE BOOKS LTD

This book is for my father, Issy Shindler

SPHERE BOOKS LTD

Published by the Penguin Group
27 Wrights Lane, London w8 5tz, England
Viking Penguin Inc., 40 West 23rd Street, New York, New York 10010, USA
Penguin Books Australia Ltd, Ringwood, Victoria, Australia
Penguin Books Canada Ltd, 2801 John Street, Markham, Ontario, Canada l3r 1b4
Penguin Books (NZ) Ltd, 182–190 Wairau Road, Auckland 10, New Zealand

Penguin Books Ltd, Registered Offices: Harmondsworth, Middlesex, England

First published in Great Britain by Sphere Books Ltd, 1988

Made and printed in Great Britain by
Richard Clay Ltd, Bungay, Suffolk

CHAPTER ONE

The prospect lay invitingly in front of Buster. He could see the golden sands shading almost into white as they approached the gentle lapping waters of the Pacific – or was it the Atlantic? The distant shouts of frolicking children barely ruffled his composure as he turned on his side and reached lazily for the champagne bottle; its cold neck sprouting from the ice bucket felt enjoyably cool against his hot skin. As he raised himself to pour the champagne he stared hard at the attractive couple lying twenty yards away on the beach.

'She can't be more than nineteen,' mused Buster, his admiration of her dark-skinned beauty in no way diminished by the proximity of her handsome, well-muscled male escort. At that moment the girl shifted her position. She opened her eyes and caught Buster's gaze. Her generous mouth opened wide in a dazzling smile.

Buster felt a warm glow of gratitude. He tried to keep a grip on his imagination as he forced himself to contemplate why these beautiful girls never seemed to bear the marks of a confrontation with a National Health Service dentist. He sank back onto his sun lounger and concentrated on feeling the heat of the noonday sun penetrate every pore in his body. A line from *The Flowerpot Men*, the television programme he watched every Wednesday with Nicky, ran through his mind in a constant refrain.

'And there they all lay, basking quietly in the sunshine . . .' But instead of the inopportune return of the Gardener from his dinner, Buster's tranquillity was shattered by a chorus of car horns and an explosion of the sort of language which rarely found its way onto British television – even after the end of *Watch with Mother*.

'Come on, mate. Can't wait here all day.'

Buster shook himself out of his romantic reverie and back into the mundane London of reality. He stumbled out of the black cab and into the murky drizzle of a May morning outside Waterloo Station. Behind him, other taxis trying to get into the station approach road were volubly manifesting their frustration at their way being blocked by Buster's idling cab. One of them tried to manoeuvre its way round Buster's taxi in order to deposit its apoplectic passenger as fast as possible but almost inevitably it was met head-on by another one coming the other way.

Meanwhile, Buster, the collar of his only decent suit turned up inadequately against the all-pervasive drizzle, examined the flowers on the stall in front of him, oblivious of the cacophony breaking out around him.

'Need a wreath,' he said to the seedy flower-seller, eyeing his wares critically.

'Yeh. You look a bit poorly,' retorted the man, his repartee honed to a fine if limited point after standing outside Waterloo Station since 1945.

Buster ignored the smart reply and patted his pockets, looking for some evidence of petty cash after what he started to remember had been a singularly unsuccessful night's gambling. The flower-seller rolled his eyes and moved to sell a large bunch of daffodils to a woman in a headscarf impatiently jingling two half-crowns together.

By the time he returned Buster had discovered a crumpled five-pound note in his trouser pocket which he brandished triumphantly.

'Still got no wreaths,' pointed out the flower-seller.

'Don't matter. I'll take them,' said Buster, pointing at a bucket of red and white carnations.

'Can't change that fiver. Only just come on.'

Buster paused as he toyed with the idea of pushing the flower-seller (whom he knew for a fact had started two hours ago) through the back of his stall and then stamping on his wares. Instead he contented himself with an airy wave of the hand as he dismissed the five-pound note from his presence.

'Just wrap them carnations for me.'

The man, grumbling, did so and as Buster leaped into his taxi with the flowers and disappeared into the enveloping maw of London's traffic, he slipped the five-pound note into the bundle of twelve single pound notes he kept securely in the small bag he wore strapped round his waist. The money bag had a sensuous feel to it. The knowledge of its existence and its physical proximity gave him an inner warmth. He turned to meet his next customer with a cheerful smile.

The funeral was nearly over. The early promise of a glorious spring morning had already given way to the inexorable passage of ever thickening grey clouds scudding across the sky. The cemetery was small but surprisingly ornate, its oldest gravestones still bearing testimony to the religious certainties of Victorian England. The surprise lay in its location – barely fifty yards from Balham High Street, one of the busiest of the South London suburbs that fanned outwards from Waterloo and Vauxhall.

Bruce Reynolds looked at Tony Sears's coffin as it inched its way into the grave. He remembered its occupant as a loser and wondered what had possessed him to decide to work with him even that one time.

The man's nerve had failed and Bruce and the gang had only just made it safely from the wrecked getaway car before the Humber with the flashing blue light had arrived. Tony was in no condition to resist arrest or to deny complicity in the post office raid. Bruce's chief memory of the affair was the purely fortuitous arrival of the taxi that took the four of them to the lock-up garage where the other car was waiting. He shuddered when he thought of the damage that could have been done to his growing reputation as one of South London's smartest crooks. He had known Tony wouldn't survive the five-year sentence. His wife had already made her feelings clear at the prospect of Tony's returning to work less than three months after being released with an already-diagnosed weak heart. Bruce saw the grieving widow turn the first shovel of dirt and repeated to himself his fervent desire never to end his days as a penniless, pathetic recidivist. Bruce reckoned he had about ten good years left in him as a top-class thief. By the time he was forty he wanted to be through with all this, having made his pile. The property market appealed to him – or maybe the film industry. He'd met enough people in show business who liked their danger by association, which they got from mixing with thieves in West End clubs, to know that he could master that racket sooner rather than later.

Bruce's contemplation of his future was abruptly halted by the approaching reverberating sound of a broken exhaust back-firing madly. Buster's taxi crested the brow of the hill and stopped fifty yards from the graveside. The mourners all turned to watch Buster stumble from the taxi, laden with inappropriate flowers, and have a short altercation with the driver which ended with Buster raising two bunches of carnations at him in a bizarre gesture of

4

defiance. The driver pointed to his meter and re-trieved his *Daily Mirror* which he started to read with exaggerated concentration.

Meanwhile Buster, beaming brightly, paid his respects to the stony-faced widow and her family as they passed him en route for the large black Wolseley that stood waiting for them near the cemetery gates. Bruce, Harry Stenford and Ronnie Biggs were still waiting for him by the grave so he shuffled over to them and tossed the flowers in a heap onto the carefully laid wreaths.

'Good timing, Buster,' grinned Harry, the amiable 6-foot 4-inch gorilla.

'Sorry, Bruce,' apologized Buster. 'Got held up at the tables.'

Bruce nodded, knowing perfectly well that Buster's idea of an all-night casino would have been some back room in a whorehouse in Bayswater, but not needing to score points off his old friend, he refrained from comment. Instead he inclined his head in the direction of the tall fair-haired man waiting patiently behind them, a lightweight raincoat over one arm.

'What's he doing here?' asked Buster anxiously.

'Showing a bit of respect for the dead. Shame you couldn't have done the same.'

'Hello, Bruce. Buster.' The man with the raincoat nodded easily at the four villains.

'Morning, Mr Mitchell,' they replied with various degrees of enthusiasm. Jack Mitchell's fame as a straight but successful copper had spread even beyond his own manor.

'What brings you to these parts?' asked Bruce, voicing all their fears.

'Same as you. I sent Tony Sears down that last time. Only right and proper I show up.'

The others were silent; Bruce and Buster thinking

what a rarity a straight copper was; Ronnie and Harry wondering whether Mitchell now knew who Tony's colleagues had been on that last job and whether the time was legally past when they could be arrested.

'Can I give you a lift to the station, Mr Mitchell?' offered Bruce in an attempt to wind things up as speedily as possible. Mitchell declined with thanks and walked briskly towards his car waiting discreetly outside the cemetery gates.

The others breathed a sigh of relief and set off for Bruce's gleaming second-hand S-type Jaguar. Buster hung back, his thoughts now racing ahead to the inevitable confrontation with June. He had promised her faithfully he wouldn't touch the rent money but the discovery of a new club in Peckham had proved too great a temptation. The funny thing was he had only taken it because he knew it was going to be a lucky night for him – he just knew it. He remembered the exact moment that the little metallic ball had flipped into the number seven groove – the sense of utter amazement rather than the loss, the feeling that it was a mistake and the spin would be replayed, the last despairing cling to the thought that maybe it was all just a nightmare, the final crushing realisation that it wasn't.

Buster dismissed the offer of a lift from Bruce and gestured nonchalantly at the taxi with the broken exhaust still idling pointedly.

'Thought I'd go home in style,' said Buster, hoping the others would take the hint. The others exchanged patronising smiles of understanding and left him to his 'glory'.

'You got a peace offering for your old lady?' Harry couldn't resist the jibe and didn't wait for a reply. Buster searched for a quick retort but it wouldn't come. It was only too true. He loved his wife deeply, had always done so ever since they had met as teenagers fifteen years earlier. Though as quick as the next villain to display his machismo, he always knew that his love for June was in complete contradiction. He was careful never to make the point too public but ironically none of his colleagues admired Buster the less for his 'handicap', and although none of them would admit it, some had a sneaking regard for a love as durable as Buster's and June's.

Still June, though a wonderful woman in many ways, was likely to be just the tiniest bit unreasonable if he went home totally empty-handed. Buster gazed at the freshly dug grave and flowers laid on it. He saw the mourners' car leaving the cemetery. Muttering an apology to his newly interred former colleague, Buster scooped up an armful of flowers and wreaths and made for his taxi. Tony would understand. He would have done the same had their positions been reversed, and Buster felt positive that his own ghost would have been generous with his floral tributes.

Buster lived in one of those anonymous terraced streets in South London that the residents bemoaned hadn't been laid waste by the Luftwaffe – at any rate after the war was over. For Buster and June it was at least better than sharing with June's mother in the new tower block she had been moved into by the council. If ever their relationship had been near to cracking it had been during the first year of life with the baby when, at the women's insistence, they had moved into the flat together. Even the mean rooms of their current dwelling were better than that. Anyway it was only temporary. June understood that. He had that meeting with the Ulsterman to go to that week and the inside information was that the Irishman was completely reliable. It was a mark of some distinction that of all the London firms, Bruce and Buster had been singled out to receive this cast-iron certainty.

'Just one decent break,' Buster thought to himself, 'that's all I need. Then it's South America, Australia, sea and sun and the good life.' He could almost taste the surf and the martinis on his lips.

The cab hooted at two boys playing football in the street. They parted reluctantly and gave a V-sign to the taxi's disappearing rear. Buster flexed his lips, preparing his devastating smile of charm, his 'little boy lost' expression, carefully rearranging the odd assortment of wreaths into a welcoming floral display. June, hearing the taxi door bang shut, flung open the front door, her eyes widening at Buster's armful of flowers, and stood there beaming, ready for an announcement of the winnings. Buster stood facing her, beaming back. Meanwhile the meter was ticking away remorselessly.

CHAPTER TWO

Buster drove carefully through the narrow streets of Camden Town, partly because the car was stolen and he didn't want to attract unnecessary attention, and partly because he wasn't too sure where he was going. Though it was barely five miles from his own front door Buster regarded North and West London as hostile areas. In South London and to a lesser extent in the East End he and Bruce were kings of their own territory or 'respected' visitors, but north and west of Marble Arch they didn't care to be seen too often. Bruce, indeed, felt more at home on the French Riviera which he and Franny had visited twice in the last two winters than he did in the environs of Kentish Town.

Buster could be quite eloquent on the subject of the deprived areas of South London. 'You ever notice that even the bleedin' Tube lines is biased?'

Bruce said nothing, his mind engaged fully with the impending meeting with the Ulsterman.

'The Northern Line is the only one what really goes south of the river and that stops at Morden. It's a disgrace. We pay the same rates and taxes as them Yids and poufs in Hampstead,' he propounded. 'How come we don't get the same service?'

Bruce looked at him shortly. 'You don't pay no taxes – nor rates. What you on about?'

'It's the principle of the thing,' said Buster doggedly.

Bruce looked at the signpost. 'Why we going towards Highgate?'

Twenty minutes later than planned Buster and Bruce found the appropriate area of Finsbury Park. They walked briskly past the football matches, the old men playing bowls and the mothers airing themselves and their small children, towards the bench on which their quarry was sitting. For a man who was carrying the secrets of a possible multi-million-pound robbery he seemed ordinary enough – slightly balding, middle-aged and wearing a shabby fawn raincoat. Bruce and Buster sat down on either side of him without formal greeting.

He continued to watch the boys playing football for a few moments. 'Good left foot that young lad's got,' he observed in his distinctive lilting voice.

'Yeh,' affirmed Buster, trying to be helpful.

'Don't listen to him. He watches Charlton Athletic,' said Bruce, trying to warn Buster to shut up and listen.

'I like watching the kids.'

Buster and Bruce exchanged glances.

'When they play in the professional game they lose something. There's too much money in the game these days. What's that Johnny Haynes earning? Hundred quid a week, isn't it? Ridiculous.'

'There's other ways of making a living of course,' said Bruce, trying to steer the conversation back on the right path. 'We was told you had some information about trains.'

The Ulsterman got up and began to walk. Bruce and Buster hurried after him. When they were out of hearing range the Ulsterman began to talk. He spoke for five minutes without interruption. The information was delivered precisely, unsensationally and in great detail. Times, security, escape routes, collection places. The Ulsterman seemed to know everything about the Royal Mail train. They would get one chance to rob it. That would be on the night of August Bank Holiday. When he had finished, Bruce asked quietly how much he thought the train would be carrying that night. 'I can't be sure exactly. My estimate is anything up to a million pounds.'

Bruce and Buster drove back in almost total silence. Each was staggered at the Ulsterman's tale. After all the years of fantasizing they were finally facing the prospect they had always dreamed of – one big haul that would enable them to 'retire' and fulfil all their dreams. Bruce thought about the travel he could afford to indulge in, the far-off places he had never seen but had longed to visit – Bali, Rio, Acapulco, Hollywood, New York, Buenos Aires. There was also the little matter of fame. Like all criminals, he maintained a somewhat ambivalent attitude towards newspaper notoriety. On the one hand it was clearly unwelcome when the heat was on, but on the other it was comforting to think of all his friends and associates reading about him on the front page.

Buster's mind was elsewhere. He enjoyed the fruits of his labours in conventionally selfish fashion but he also loved to fling money on the kitchen table, to peel off notes from a large wad and hand them to June with a nonchalant air, to come home unexpectedly laden with gifts for June and their three-year-old daughter, Nicky. With the proceeds of this mail train robbery Buster could now seriously start thinking about a large detached house, perhaps in the Surrey stockbroker belt near Reigate or Surbiton. There would be private education for the children, trips abroad, nowhere too flashy, maybe the Channel Islands or the South of France. Bruce was always on about the South of France. Apparently all the girls sunbathed topless, but that was probably just another one of Bruce's stories, trying to wind him up.

The familiar traffic snarl-up at the Elephant and Castle brought both of them back to reality. They talked in low tones of the implications of the Ulsterman's information. There was clearly a need for thorough preparation and planning down to the minutest detail. Bruce thought another firm would have to be brought in to provide back-up and additional expertise, but Buster was adamantly opposed to this. The prospect of sharing any of the million-pound haul was anathema to him. They did agree, however, to consult Harry, Ronnie and other members of their own firm before making a definite decision. Buster told Bruce he would personally see Harry the following morning, and dropped off his partner by his carefully-parked, gleaming, second-hand Ford Zephyr.

Buster's mind raced as it absorbed the new information. Even watching *Rawhide*, his favourite televison programme, his attention wandered from the screen to the new scenario taking place in his brain. June, who had tried five times to tell him about a house she had seen in the estate agent's window, finally lost her patience and stood directly in front of the television set.

'What? What?' shouted Buster, his attention finally secured.

'Why can't we buy that house?'

'What house?' he asked, genuinely puzzled.

'That house,' she replied, pointing to the estate agent's sheet on his lap. 'The one I've been trying to get you to talk about ever since you came home. I can't go on hiding behind the couch every time the rent man calls. We've got another baby on the way.'

Buster hated these conversations. June's persistent desire for some form of security ran counter to the grandiloquent ideas Buster had for providing for his family. In a funny sort of way he quite enjoyed hiding from the rent man. So had June once upon a time. However this latest pregnancy coming on top of two earlier miscarriages seemed to have taken all the old bravado out of June.

On the screen a very young Clint Eastwood was looking sadly at the dead body of a beautiful homesteader. In South London Buster was trying to decide whether to tell June about the prospective windfall of the train robbery or go down to the pub as a statement of masculine pride. In the event he was permitted neither as June pressed home her attack and her desire to be a home-owner. Buster tried arguing rationally, pointing out that the amount necessary for the deposit, let alone the price of the house, was beyond them at the moment. He started to describe the boundless riches that might be theirs by the summer but June clearly wasn't interested. All she could see was the prospect of having her husband in jail when the new baby was born. Buster protested that throughout his career he had been blessed with good luck, but this failed to move his implacable wife.

'And what happens when you ain't so lucky? Where do the baby clothes come from then?'

And thus it was that Buster Edwards, embryonic Great Train Robber, found himself on a wet spring night, breaking and entering the premises of the local Mothercare and purloining a dozen Babygros, two dozen terry-towelling nappies, a large box of talcum powder, a pair of cot sheets, two feeding bottles, half a dozen rubber teats and a potty.

CHAPTER THREE

The serious planning got under way as soon as Bruce and Buster had checked out what they could of the Ulsterman's story. They paid twopence each to get onto the platform at Euston Station. There they watched the mounds of high-value packages being loaded onto the second coach of the mail train precisely as the Irishman had told them.

Nobody had ever held up a train before and they all knew it would take considerable work before the August deadline to ensure they were ready. Bruce and Buster decided they needed to practise. They avoided the Euston line on which the Royal Mail ran and settled on the Southern Region which ran from Victoria to the South Coast. A few days of scouting told them where to place the getaway car, and the robbers went to work.

Buster sat patiently on the toilet awaiting a knock on the door from Harry. As soon as it came he pulled the communication cord. The train slithered to a halt barely yards from the spot the robbers had pinpointed. While a bemused guard wandered up and down the train looking for the cause of the disturbance, Harry, Buster and Bruce slipped quietly off the train over the fence and into the waiting car on the road. They sang raucously all the way home.

The following Friday they tried again, this time with the intention of actually removing some of the high-value packages. Thanks to the Ulsterman, they knew that HVPs were always to be found in the last sack loaded onto the train and were identified with a distinctive pink label.

Between Horsley and Lewes, Bruce and Harry knocked on the toilet door and made their way towards the baggage car. Buster pulled the communication cord as arranged but for some reason, which they never found out, the train failed to stop. Bruce and Harry had already tied up the baggage car attendant so they were half-way through the robbery before they realized that something had gone wrong. Buster, swearing imaginatively, jerked frantically at the communication cord and eventually, to his relief, the brakes were applied and the train started to slow. In the baggage van Bruce and Harry had a brief shouting match about how many HVPs they could take with them.

Buster unlocked the toilet and started to climb down from the train. To his consternation there was no sign of either his friends or the getaway car which had observed the train speeding past the pre-arranged spot and assumed initially that the train it was waiting for was late. Meanwhile the menacing-looking fireman had climbed down from his cab and was heading towards Buster.

At this moment Harry and Bruce dropped the HVP sack onto the line and jumped down after it. The fireman set off towards them at a run. The robbers scrambled through the dense hedgerows and found themselves on a pleasant Sussex country lane with only a retired couple from Blackburn, out for a stroll before lunch as company.

Meanwhile the driver of Bruce's Jaguar, realizing that the train he was supposed to be meeting had stopped a mile up the road, had set off in pursuit of his friends, only to find himself at an unfamiliar fork in the road. Inevitably he had chosen the wrong one and was desperately retracing his steps when he was confronted by a dishevelled Bruce and Buster shouting frantically. He screeched to a halt and the two men got in and looked back to see Harry and the fireman locked in a grim struggle for possession of the HVP sack. Just as they were imploring him to drop it and scramble in, Harry wrenched himself free of his opponent's grip and jabbed him painfully in the solar plexus. Winded, the man lay there helplessly as Harry put the boot in and finished him off. The car reversed at top speed, picked up Harry and his lovingly-cradled booty and roared off in search of the A23.

The reward for such strenuous effort proved disappointingly small. There were no precious stones as they had hoped and very few of the small hard packages that contained the surplus banknotes being sent to the central clearing banks in the City. It was time to call in the experts. Even Buster agreed this time.

The meeting took place a few days later in a room above the Crown and Mitre in Lambeth. There were fifteen men and three crates of beer crowded uneasily together in a room ill designed to meet their needs, and dense with the congealed smog of heavy-tar cigarette smoke. Bruce tried to act as the smiling diplomat, making the unnecessary introductions, but he couldn't dispel the cloud of suspicion through which each firm regarded the other. Both had their origins in the slum dwellings of Vauxhall, Kennington and Lambeth but the Crown and Mitre was Bruce's and Buster's territory and all the men knew it.

The second firm was led by George, a small, wiry, cunning individual who sat in silence, neither smoking nor drinking, merely cradling a box on his lap. George had recently acquired a reputation in the underworld for successful if relatively small-time robberies from trains. He had not actually stopped a train so far, but rumour was current that he possessed the means to do so, and all eyes were fixed on his box as if it held the proceeds of the Royal Mail train.

The negotiations, when they got under way, were a mixture of bravado and accusation. Buster, Harry and Ronnie regarded the second firm's demands as extortionate, and it took all Bruce's considerable prowess at negotiating to prevent the outbreak of violence with which such discussions were frequently punctuated. Eventually it was recognized that a percentage split of a potential haul of five million pounds left a little to spare, even after deducting the combined aggregate of the robbers' avarice.

Once the most contentious issues were settled, the heat went out of the atmosphere. Discussion proceeded to planning the robbery itself and all the details that a raid of this scope and daring inevitably entailed. There were fears expressed that working outside London was unlucky and that someone was bound to be nicked.

'It's difficult to persuade British Railways to bring the train into the pub. We got to go and get it ourselves,' said Bruce with a touch of impatience.

George, who knew the mechanics of the railways better than anyone else present, laid down what he thought were the primary needs when planning the exact location of the heist. He could only stop the train at the set of signals suspended from the gantry. They therefore had to find a gantry that was close to a bridge so that the train could be quickly brought to a position from which the heavy mailbags could be speedily unloaded, rolled down the embankment, tossed into the lorries and driven off.

'What about after?' wondered one of George's henchmen. 'We all doing the split here or what?'

Bruce grinned. This was his moment. 'I been thinking about that. Very dangerous, bunch of villains wandering round town with a million quid. We do the job Wednesday night, shit hits the fan Thursday morning. We stay there, under wraps, till Sunday. We do the split there and nobody, repeat nobody, leaves till Sunday. Old Bill will all assume we split up. There won't be a single lead back to us.'

There was a pause while the magnitude of what Bruce was suggesting sank in. Usually, no matter how far away the job the basic belief of all London thieves was to get back to the city and safety as fast as possible. They felt conspicuous in the country and uncomfortable in any other city for more than a few days. At home in the pubs and back streets of the city, protected by an army of friends, relatives and a working-class solidarity that had no affinity with the forces of law and order they felt safe. Bruce was asking them to forego that sense of security just at the time they all felt they needed it the most.

'We'll have to talk about it,' said George, reluctant to commit his gang to the plan without consultation. 'So where's the hiding place?'

Bruce and Buster exchanged glances. Despite many miles of happy motoring with Esso and other brands, they had failed so far to find any hiding place that offered anything like the anonymity they sought. 'We'll let you know, soon as you tell us you agree to the deal,' said Bruce, wrenching back the upper hand.

The next week Buster and Bruce were back on the trail of the Royal Mail train. Following the Ordnance Survey map purchased from W. H. Smith, the two men followed the railway line all the way from Rugby in the Midlands until it entered the London conurbation near Wembley. In particular they examined the Hertfordshire section between Watford and Berkhamsted but the viaducts were either too high or not sufficiently removed from outlying houses for them to be able to operate within the safety margin they needed.

Beyond Berkhamsted, a town to which Buster unaccountably took violent exception as he watched the effete middle classes in their natural habitat, the nature of the countryside began to change. Buster had carefully marked all the potential bridges on the map and eventually they found that bridge no. 127, also known as Bridego Bridge, was perfect for their purposes. It spanned a narrow but generally deserted country road and the distance from the railway line to the road level was only about fifteen feet. It would take only eight or ten men to form an efficient chain. More to the point, it was only about half a mile from the requisite set of signals suspended from the gantry at Sears Crossing. About three-quarters of a mile further north was the back-up signal that would have to be set to amber while Sears Crossing was turned to red.

Bruce and Buster returned to the car well satisfied with their morning's work. They now knew where the Great Train Robbery was to take place.

Next day they returned with the somewhat sceptical George, still clutching his box of tricks. Despite his unwillingness to be seen to betray too much enthusiasm, George had to admit that Bridego Bridge and Sears Crossing were perfect for their purposes.

'I can stop the train, old son. Can you get it to the bridge?'

'If you can stop it we can shift it,' challenged Buster.

'How?' asked George.

'Push it if we have to,' came the unilluminating reply.

'You tell us how you're going to stop it,' said Bruce, still probing for the information that George had so far not deigned to reveal.

'My job is to stop it. How I do it's my business.' George was clearly determined to go to his grave with the secret of his box still with him. Buster toyed briefly with the idea of punching all his teeth in. George decided to deflect any further discussion by pointing out to Bruce that he would still have to un-couple the engine and the two front cars from the rest of the train and move them forward, thereby stranding the seventy ordinary sorters, which would leave only the six sorters in the HVP coach and of course the train driver and his fireman to deal with.

The would-be train robbers approached their task with the methodical application that the professional Bruce had tried hard to instil into them. Three of them actually got casual labouring jobs in the railway yards near Wembley so that they could examine the HVP coaches and their locks in great detail. They learned how to uncouple coaches and what it took to shunt an engine. Night after night, to June's irritation, Bruce and Buster would wait by Bridego Bridge until they saw the pin-pricks of light from the narrow windows of the Royal Mail train. If it was on time it would flash through Sears Crossing shortly after 3 am. The two men then drove carefully all over the quiet, narrow country roads of South Oxford-shire, Bedfordshire and North Hertfordshire to gauge the normal amount of traffic they were likely to meet at that time in the morning.

The one crucial item of importance they failed to acquire, however, was the exact location of their hide-away. As the days slipped by it was not only George's boys who started to get anxious at the delayed an-nouncement. 'For Christ's sake, Bruce,' snapped Harry, 'there's only seven weeks left and we still don't know where we're going.'

'Have faith,' replied Bruce shortly.

Everywhere they went Bruce seemed to find an ob-jection: it was too far from Bridego Bridge and the dangers of being intercepted were too great; or there were farms in the vicinity that might produce an unwelcome friendly visit; or they were too near the main road and they wouldn't get a clear sight of the police if they had to evacuate suddenly. The longer this search for perfection went on the more nervous everyone became, especially Buster who was getting considerable aggravation from June at these frequent absences from the marital bed. There was a long-standing arrangement between Buster and June that he only volunteered the information he wanted her to hear and she never pried into areas that she accepted were none of her business. It wasn't as if she had no idea where the money was coming from that fed and clothed them; it was simply safer for both their sakes that she didn't become privy to the sort of information that could land her in trouble if Buster were ever taken.

The finding of the safe house, however, was something different. Buster had never worked on any enterprise as grandiose as the Royal Mail job nor on any job that took him out of London for so long. The date of Buster and June's anniversary was approaching and they had agreed they would leave Nicky with June's mother for the day and spend it somewhere together.

'I need you, Buster,' said Bruce the day before. 'Your anniversary will still be there next year. This job won't. Just tell her you're working.'

Buster became increasingly uncomfortable. He hated these battles between Bruce and June for his loyalty. Usually he managed to keep the two of them in separate compartments of his life but when they spilled over into each other as they had now, the mess was horrible.

'For God's sake, Bruce, one day, that's all I'm talking about. One lousy, stinking day. I'll be back on

Friday. I just want this day for June and me. You ain't paying my wages you know.' Bruce said nothing but raised his eyebrows.

The day of the anniversary was spent combing the lanes between Thame and Aylesbury.

'Very picturesque,' commented Bruce as the feeble sunshine poked its way through the white cloud cover. 'You don't get the brilliance of the Riviera in England. Even in the height of summer.'

Buster had nothing to add to the conversation. Bruce, the only one of his acquaintances who had been abroad more than once, always emphasised his cultural superiority when he wanted to make a point.

Buster looked at his watch. It was now nearly 6.30 pm and he had faithfully promised June he would be back by 8 o'clock at the latest so they could still go out for the evening. They were standing outside a detached cottage with a 'For Sale' sign stuck in the ground outside. Bruce was visually measuring the distance from the house to the road and the amount of time they would have to slip away at the back if the police came nosing around. He was like a golfer sizing up the difficulties of the decisive putt on the eighteenth green. Finally but decisively Bruce shook his head.

'Oh, for Christ's sake! Wassamarrer with this one?'

'Too close to that house over there.'

'Bollocks!' averred Buster. 'Who's gonna be watching?'

'You're getting sloppy, Buster. June waiting for you to clock in, is she?'

Buster, expertly needled by Bruce, exploded on cue. 'Piss off, Bruce. Just 'cause I prefer her company to yours sometimes. Specially when you're being an aggravating sod like you are now.'

Satisfied with his moral victory, Bruce got back

22

into the car, turned on the ignition and pulled on the starter button. The Jaguar roared into life. Buster consulted the map on his knee.

'Just turn left at that crossroads.'

'That just takes you straight back to Aylesbury,' Bruce pointed out.

'No, it don't. That's south towards London. I been watching.'

'You?' expostulated Bruce. 'You can't find your way north of Billingsgate Market – even with a map.'

'For Christ's sake, Bruce. Just listen to me for once in your life. Now turn left there and put your foot down.'

Bruce delayed the turn as long as possible then wrenched at the steering-wheel and turned left almost on two wheels. The natural pallor of Buster's complexion was exaggerated by a series of high-speed turns which left his stomach hanging from his mouth. The wild ride was finally halted as Bruce, seeing yet another 'For Sale' sign, swung the car to the right and disappeared from the main road up a winding dirt-track of 200 yards, screeching to a stop outside a deserted farmhouse.

Bruce got out of the car and a broad smile creased his features as he turned this way and that.

'Must be, what, thirty miles from the bridge. And the view! We'd be able to see Old Bill for miles and them trees'll probably hide us from most places on the road.' He turned to Buster spontaneously, grabbed him and kissed him on the top of his head. 'You balding little genius. You may have very little hair but you have an enormous brain, my son. Look at it. Just look at the bleeder!'

Buster struggled free with as much dignity as he could muster. 'Yeh,' he said nonchalantly. 'I reckon that's it.'

They had found Leatherslade Farm.

CHAPTER FOUR

The one remaining problem was solved by, of all people, Ronnie Biggs. Biggs had originally met Bruce in the salubrious surroundings of Wandsworth Prison where they discovered that they shared similar interests in jazz, Hemingway and fantasies of a professional as well as a sexual nature. Bruce, however, was serious and successful about it all. Ronnie Biggs's attempts to become a master criminal declined rapidly, to the extent that he was eventually incarcerated for eighteen months for the big-time job of taking and driving away a Morris Minor without its owner's consent.

For the past year or so Biggs had actually been working as a handyman and carpenter in Surrey. It turned out to be more profitable for him to overcharge the bourgeoisie for his legitimate services than to attempt to relieve them of their more valuable possessions. Though Bruce recognized Biggs's lack of flair he felt that Biggs was at least reliable and had a sense of personal loyalty. With so much money at stake, loyalty was an asset not to be lightly disregarded.

During the course of an evening's conversation, Biggs revealed that he was now renovating the small house of a retired train driver. Interest instantly aroused, Bruce probed a little deeper. The moment Biggs sensed that Bruce was about to involve him on a 'proper' job he started to inflate the old man's abilities.

'Could he drive one of them big diesels?' Bruce wanted to know.

'Course he could,' volunteered Biggs immediately.

'Would he ever do anything dodgy?' wondered Bruce.

Biggs explained that the old man was getting a British Railways' pension of three pounds a week. He was using most of his savings to redecorate the house.

'For ten grand he'd drive a space rocket,' opined Biggs.

Thus it was that Ronnie Biggs's old man became the missing piece of the jigsaw puzzle. He would be the man to replace the driver of the Royal Mail when it was stopped at Sears Crossing, and would drive the engine and HGV coach the three-quarters of a mile down the track to Bridego Bridge. Ronnie Biggs crowed with delight. He was back where he wanted to be – playing with the big boys. No more new shelves in the study and more cupboard space above the cooker for him. As for all of them, the dream of unimaginable wealth danced in front of his eyes.

The dream had started to punctuate the conversations between Buster and June. The prospect of a five-million-pound haul was the realization of everybody's fantasies. Retirement to a large house where June would have every electrical kitchen gadget they could buy at Harrods was supplemented by Buster's recurring vision of a tropical paradise where cold drinks and a large villa intermingled with the warmth of the sun and the omnipresence of pretty girls. Quite how June fitted into the latter fantasy Buster never quite resolved, but he knew that if this train job came off they were made for life. Admittedly June didn't like the idea of abroad. She was very close to her mother and her friends and felt uncomfortable out of her traditional milieu. But Buster knew he could cure that. A couple of hundred thousand pounds would cure all that, that was for sure.

'Just think, £200,000. That's more than Spurs paid to A.C. Milan for Jimmy Greaves.'

As the days slipped by during the cool and showery July of 1963 June saw fewer and fewer flashes of the Buster who had raced back from a scouting job with Bruce to take her to see *Lawrence of Arabia* at the Odeon. He punctuated his conversation with references to 'the dream' which June chose steadfastly to ignore. She recognized the signs of an impending job, which always concerned her but at least it had been a consistent feature of their married life. This time, however, Buster was mentally withdrawing from her still further, becoming disturbingly moody and silent. June was now in her fifth month of pregnancy and with a history of miscarriages behind her, before the successful birth of Nicky three years before, she was more apprehensive than usual. It bothered her to see her husband, normally so sunny and uncomplicated, fall a victim to emotional gloom.

In the car on the way to her mother's, June started to probe about the length of Buster's projected absence.

'How long, Buster? Mum's bound to ask.'

'Tell her what you always tell her,' replied Buster irritably. He drove on through Kennington and round the semi-circle at the Oval that ran from the Pavilion to Vauxhall Road. A large crowd of eager bodies was emerging from the tube station and hurrying towards the turnstiles under the famous gasometers. 'There must be a match on,' thought June, envying for the moment the happiness of the family unity displayed so blatantly in front of her. Boys' hands inside their fathers', occasionally with a mother trailing behind them carrying the bag with the plastic mackintoshes and the freshly cut sandwiches.

'Maybe being ordinary isn't too bad,' she speculated to herself. The imminent arrival of another baby had changed her thinking somewhat, making her much less relaxed about the way Buster usually provided for the family.

Recent attempts to discuss practical things like houses invariably met with complete dismissal from Buster. When June had provoked him by forcing him to think about what life would be like for her without him with two young mouths to feed and a new baby to clothe, Buster's immediate response had been to rob Mothercare. In fact that hadn't been such a bad night. Buster had returned like Santa Claus with a sack of toys and baby stuff over his shoulder. Hurling himself onto the bed after the merchandise he and June had enjoyed one of their very best times in bed. A job and its attendant dangers always sent a shot of adrenalin through Buster. He needed it to prove to himself that he was alive and its effect on him was quite remarkable. June warmed inwardly as she recalled the aftermath of the Mothercare theft. She wanted that warm and loving Buster. When he was like that he was the most exciting man in the world to her. He was, admittedly, somewhat overweight for the traditional image of a great lover, being a little too fond of alcohol and a diet in which fried foods and chips featured heavily, but this was the man June had taken for better or worse and she had no real desire to change her mind just now.

Buster turned into the courtyard of the tower block and switched off the engine. He turned to his wife and took her tenderly in his arms, the warmth and sincerity of his action being a hundredfold more articulate than he could ever be with mere words. June returned his kiss with feeling.

'Take care of yourself, won't you?' she said, anxious not to betray too much emotion.

'Don't I always?'

June looked at him, equally unable to express her deepest thoughts in words, although after fifteen years together Buster had a fairly shrewd idea what was going on behind those pretty eyes. Once again he repeated his belief. 'I'm doing this for all of us.'

June nodded and Buster confirmed he would keep in touch in the usual way, knowing perfectly well that if it went according to plan June would know everything the moment she picked up a newspaper on the Thursday morning.

Mrs Barker appeared as the two of them embraced again. They sprang apart. Somehow, even after fifteen years of marriage, they didn't like to be seen displaying physical affection in public. The time they had spent living with Mrs Barker had nearly destroyed their sex life altogether.

June got out of the car, carrying Nicky and the small suitcase she always took with her. Nicky was swept up in her grandmother's arms and Buster seized the moment to swing the car around and shout his farewells. Not stopping to indulge in yet another circuitous conversation with Mrs Barker, Buster drove dangerously fast out of the courtyard and into the main road without stopping or looking back. June and her mother exchanged glances but both knew that Buster was incorrigible. He came as a complete piece of merchandise. He had defied all female attempts to change him in any significant way.

'Like a cuppa?'

June nodded gratefully. Her mother might not be Buster's greatest admirer but she knew the score.

The Landrover Buster was driving had been neatly removed from its position outside the Vaudeville Theatre in the Strand by Buster and Ronnie the previous night. Harry had provided the new registration

28

plates and the pots of green paint with which it was their intention to disguise it still further once they had arrived at Leatherslade Farm.

'Takes me back a bit,' Buster had remarked as they swung easily round the Aldwych and over Waterloo Bridge. It was the maximum amount of nostalgia Buster was prepared to confess. Ronnie kept quiet, unwilling to admit to a much more recent spate of low-status car thefts.

They picked up Bruce and Harry as arranged and then Ronnie directed them to the house of Old Walter, the man who was to drive the train that crucial mile or so down the track to Bridego Bridge. The meeting was not propitious. They had relied, against Harry's better judgment, entirely on Ronnie to vouch for the old man. None of the gang other than Ronnie had ever seen Walter before so it was with some trepidation that they saw him now on the pavement in front of his house, battered suitcase at his feet, a bright smile on his face and a fishing-rod clutched in one hand. To a man they were all horrified.

'Jesus!' exclaimed Buster voicing all their thoughts. 'He thinks he's going on a bleeding holiday.'

Walter clambered awkwardly into the Landrover over Ronnie, apologized as he clobbered Bruce on the back of the head with his suitcase and then nearly poked Harry's eye out with the fishing-rod.

'Watch what you're doing with that thing,' warned Harry fiercely.

'Thought I'd get a spot of fishing in – while we're waiting,' explained Walter.

The others said nothing. They instinctively felt Biggs had landed them with a complete liability – one who would panic the moment things went wrong and who, if he were ever picked up, would be able to identify all of them to the police.

Walter settled himself eventually, grinned at his new colleagues and announced with the importance of a man who had never lied to his wife in forty years of married life, 'The wife thinks I'm off on a tree-felling expedition.'

'Oh, yeh?' said Harry sarcastically. 'Lumberjack are you?'

'Oh, no,' laughed Walter, 'I'm a bit old for that. Told her I was going with you as a tea-boy.'

The others grinned. 'You're a bit old for that too, Grandad.'

Ronnie squirmed. Old Walter was his big contribution to the preparations for the Great Train Robbery. He was aware that he wasn't greatly liked and that Bruce had had to insist on his involvement. Walter had failed to make too big an initial impression.

They all fell silent as the Landrover nosed its way out of the London traffic and out onto the A40, heading towards Denham and Gerrards Cross. Walter, equally aware that things were a bit tense, sought desperately in his mind to think of something to say that would go down well. Eventually he found it.

'Nice motor, this,' he commented. 'Whose is it?'

Ronnie replied instantly urging Walter to shut up. 'Buster and me nicked it down Vauxhall way last night.'

The old man was both shocked and alarmed. 'Nicked? You mean it's stolen? Hey, you boys want to be careful. You can get in trouble for nicking cars.'

At about the time the Landrover was turning off the main road and up the track to Leatherslade Farm June first began to notice the cramps. She had already acquired a history of miscarriages and even though Nicky had been a fine, healthy normal pregnancy and delivery neither she nor Buster relaxed much until she had carried this latest pregnancy into its fifth month.

'What's he up to this time?' asked Mrs Barker as she stirred two large spoons of white sugar into her tea.

June soon confided in her mother her fears for Buster's latest unknown adventure. 'I think it's something big. He's on about this dream all the time. How we're gonna be rich and have anything we want.'

'That'll be nice,' said her mother rather absently.

'Oh, Mum, I'm scared. He's going to try something silly and get himself nicked. I can feel it.'

Her mother made standard attempts to comfort her but once started June's fears could not be stemmed. She worried particularly because she knew, whatever the job was, it was happening outside London and both June and her mother knew of the superstition surrounding thieves who worked outside the city. Mrs Barker tried to change the conversation. 'What about the baby?'

'Oh, he provides for it all right. He's nicked stuff from every Mothercare in London!'

'No. I mean, does he want it?'

'He's got to want it,' laughed June. 'I mean, he didn't get no receipt so he can't take the clobber back, can he?'

Mrs Barker joined in the laughter and then stopped abruptly when she noticed June's face creased with the stab of pain. A quick examination showed that already a small seepage of blood was beginning to show. Quickly June got herself into bed but the cramps showed no sign of abating. It felt for all the world like the miscarriage she had had at sixteen weeks four years before. Mrs Barker sent the little boy from next door up to the surgery.

It was two hours before the doctor arrived and in

that time June, helpless in bed, felt the foetus tearing itself away from the lining of the womb. The physical pain, excrutiating though it was, was as nothing compared to the anguish and misery she felt. At the moment she felt the baby die inside her she called out for Buster.

'Well, where is he, the little bastard? He should be with his wife – a time like this.'

Instinctively June started her well-worn defence. 'He's working, Mum. Earning a living.'

'Oh, yeh? Proper little breadwinner, he is,' snapped Mrs Barker scornfully.

She was every bit as upset and helpless as June.

The doctor arrived at four o'clock to examine the extent of the damage. He clucked sympathetically and then made the same speech about Nature's desire for natural abortions that June had heard at least once before and under similar circumstances.

Just about the time Buster Edwards was sitting down at Leatherslade Farm to a game of Monopoly, his embryonic child died in the womb of its mother.

CHAPTER FIVE

Leatherslade Farm still wasn't legally in their possession when the robbers moved in. The place had not been found until the end of June and the creaky legal machinery could not be significantly accelerated, despite the urgency of the task in hand. The robbers were entirely dependent on the goodwill of the vendor to permit them to occupy the farmhouse 'for the purpose of redecoration' after contracts had been exchanged and ten per cent of the purchase price of £5550 had been paid. Completion would not take place until 13 August – a week after the robbery was due to take place.

The redecoration planned by the robbers was rudimentary to say the least. The living-room was soon decked out with curtains made from surplus army khaki blankets. It was important to keep the place blacked out. Bruce put on a pair of white overalls just prior to painting the Landrover green. It was just as well for him that he did, for no sooner was he changed than the farmer from the next holding appeared unexpectedly.

'Afternoon,' came the cheerful greeting.

'Afternoon,' replied Bruce cautiously.

'John Wyatt. Next farm. The Rixons rented me that field. I'd very much like to continue the arrangement.'

Bruce breathed a sigh of relief. 'I'm just the decorator. The new owner don't move in till we've finished.'

The farmer looked disappointed at the delay. 'Who is the new owner, then? Rixons wouldn't tell us.'

'Man called Fielding, I think. Lives in Aylesbury.'

The farmer took the news in good spirits and departed. Buster, who with Harry had been digging a large pit to bury the empty mailbags in, came round to enquire about the unexpected visitor. They all recognized the necessity to remain hidden from view and retreated indoors immediately.

The waiting seemed interminable. Since they wouldn't be leaving the farm until well after midnight most of the men had brought air mattresses which they began to blow up.

'Gives me a hard-on,' observed Ronnie Biggs.

'What the hell d'you do with your old lady if blowing up a Li-lo gives you a hard-on?' wondered Buster.

There was the inevitable outburst of ribald suggestions all of them obscene, many of them physically impossible. Biggs took the ribbing in good heart. He liked to be the centre of attention, no matter how brief the duration.

The Monopoly board which was likely to see considerable action in the days leading up to the gang's dispersal on Sunday was already in use. Those not busily engaged in buying Mayfair and Park Lane were obsessively checking their equipment. A VHF radio, which had been brought so that they could listen to the police broadcasts, was already tuned to the evening news which gave ever more extraordinary details of the mystery surrounding the suicide the previous week of Stephen Ward, the osteopath, artist and, according to several popular newspapers, High Society pimp.

At seven o'clock Bruce drove to a country road telephone box and rang the Ulsterman who confirmed that his contacts at Glasgow and Crewe had already called in to confirm that there were over one hundred high-value packages on the Royal Mail. Bruce returned to the farm and conveyed the information. There was an imperceptible quickening of the pulse for all concerned except old Walter.

'What d'you mean, it's on? Was it going to be off? Anyway who told you?'

A fierce growl arose from the assembled troops and Ronnie decided to deflect further unpleasantness by leading Walter upstairs and persuading him to stay in one of the bedrooms until the time came to leave.

As midnight struck Bruce made a tour of inspection. Once again he was living out one of his recurring fantasies – to be the youngest major in the British Army. Ironically the only item that didn't pass inspection was the pistol he found on one of George's firm. 'No shooters,' he barked, angry that his explicit orders had been disobeyed. He was quite resolved that the number of heavies he had recruited and their trusty coshes would be enough to overpower the unarmed and, hopefully, highly-surprised team of post office sorters. If anything disastrous happened and some of them were eventually taken, he knew that judges were likely to be harder on a convicted felon who had been armed than on one who was not. The Great Train Robbery was to depend on speed, surprise, detailed planning and the willingness to use force if necessary. Firearms were an irrelevance.

Half an hour after midnight the convoy rolled impressively down the rutted farm track and swung east onto the country roads that would carry it across Oxfordshire and Buckinghamshire to its rendezvous with destiny. In the front went the freshly painted Landrover, followed by a large army truck which had been legitimately bought and was designed to hold the huge numbers of mailbags. Bringing up the rear was another Landrover with most of the heavy villains on board.

The journey took just over forty minutes as they were anxious not to arouse suspicion by speeding along the lanes even though the army base at Bicester could have been used as support cover. Everyone, except George and old Walter, was dressed in battle fatigues. If they were stopped they would claim that they were on army manoeuvres.

In the event they passed no traffic at all on the way to Bridego Bridge. They now had nearly two hours to wait before the Mail Train was due. The men all had pre-arranged tasks. On arrival at the Bridge one of them was driven as far as possible up the line to the dwarf signal which would show amber. When Bruce gave the word over his walkie-talkie the man would place the large wicket-keeper's glove over the functioning green signal and connect up the amber light with leads from the batteries to crocodile clips on the bulb. At the gantry at Sears Crossing George would do the same with the red bulb.

Opposite the gantry, their bodies flattened to the embankment, lay the heavies whose job it was to persuade the driver and fireman not to interfere while old Walter was piloting the engine and the H V P coach down the track to Bridego Bridge.

If the robbers had imagined that the track would be completely empty until the Royal Mail arrived they were quickly disillusioned. The line was quite busy with its regular allotment of night-time freight traffic. One goods vehicle drew up, quite unexpectedly, directly opposite the spot where the gang of heavies was waiting. Old Walter, whose nerves were already stretched to breaking point, instinctively produced his pipe and started patting his pockets for a box of matches. Buster, alerted by the sound of the matches shaking in the half-empty box, reached across and smashed the box from Walter's trembling

36

fingers. The driver and fireman of the freight engine were near enough for them to overhear their conversation. Eventually, to everyone's relief, the goods train started to chug off again.

Bruce, from his vantage point, kept his eyes fixed on the horizon that would shortly reveal the Glasgow–London mail train. He played over in his mind for the umpteenth time the checklist of final preparations. He couldn't imagine it could go wrong at this stage. He really believed he had taken everything into consideration and as his eyes sought the tell-tale holes in the darkness for confirmation of his troops' readiness he mentally congratulated himself on the scope and daring of the feat they were shortly to accomplish. He had occasionally wondered, in one of his more reflective moments when a job hadn't gone as smoothly as had been anticipated, whether he wasn't better suited to a job in the legitimate world where planning, foresight and determination could bring their own rewards. But he knew that he could never face the long haul that legitimate enterprises seemed to demand. He had already spent winters in St Tropez and other fashionable parts of the Continent. Few legitimate concerns could give him that sort of tangible reward at the age of thirty-three, and looking around at the fifteen men neatly deployed to relieve the banks of five million pounds with the minimum of fuss, Bruce experienced a glow of pride he could only describe as job satisfaction.

His ruminations were halted by the clickety-clack sound of a train moving at high speed, borne to him through the stillness of the night. As he discerned the faint pin-pricks of light from the first carriages of the Royal Mail, Bruce shone his torch onto his watch. It was exactly 3.02 am. The train was on time. It was a good sign. Bruce picked up his walkie-talkie. His voice was deliberately, almost exaggeratedly, calm, betraying no trace of the mounting excitement and nerves leading almost to nausea that he knew he and the rest of his men were feeling.

'It's coming down, chaps. This is it.'

The dwarf signal switched to amber and the gantry turned to red. The huge diesel engine could be heard applying its brakes. The train slowed at the amber signal and drew to a stop opposite the gantry where the red light, connected to George's battery, glowed brightly in the dark. Hidden from sight along the embankment, Buster and his mates heard the voice of the irritated fireman.

'Not again! What d'you think it is this time?'

'Better get out and have a look,' came the rejoinder from the driver.

Obediently the young fireman climbed down from the cab and trotted across the tracks to the telephone on the embankment directly above where Buster and the others were waiting for him. Buster stood up and the fireman, presuming him to be a manual railway worker, simply enquired why the train was stopped.

'Well, the red's on,' said Buster, enjoying the temporary farce of the situation.

'Aye, but why's it on?'

'Dunno. Ask them down there.'

The fireman peered, puzzled, down the embankment for a moment. Buster gave him an almighty shove and the fireman was secured in the waiting arms of two of the heavies. A cosh was raised threateningly.

'It's all right. I'm on your side,' gasped the fireman quickly. The cosh remained poised over his face in case he decided to change his mind at a more convenient later date.

Buster was still struggling to climb into the cab

itself. The driver, alerted by the noise of his fireman tumbling down the embankment and coming to a muffled stop, was shocked to see a masked face trying to climb into his engine. He stood on Buster's fingers hard. Buster swore in pain and then was lifted up by Harry so that he could strike out at the driver with his cosh. Other heavies pouring into the cab from the other side quickly made the driver captive though he was inclined to be a lot less co-operative than his mate.

Old Walter's supreme moment had arrived. As if he weren't terrified enough by the spectacle of his new colleagues in their battle-dress and balaclavas, he took one look at the driver whose forehead was pouring blood from a wound caused by recent contact with a lead cosh, and nearly fainted. He was pushed to the controls of the train and, inevitably, he panicked. For all his stories of life on the big engines and Ronnie Biggs's subsequent embellishment of them, the fact remained that Old Walter had only ever worked in a shunting yard. He sat in the driver's seat, and with his foot on the safety device he turned the handles to release the brakes and move the train, but although the engine seemed to respond, it didn't move.

The gang knew precisely how long they had to get the train to the bridge, unload the mailbags and leave. Already Walter was costing them valuable seconds.

'Get the fuck out of it,' snapped Harry.

'It's the vacuum; I can't get the vacuum.'

Harry hauled the old man out of the seat by the collar and picked up the bleeding driver from the floor. 'Move this train or you'll get some more.'

The driver thought it wiser to co-operate. He coaxed the vacuum and slowly the big engine, with half the gang clinging to its outside, chugged its way forward towards Bridego Bridge.

It was difficult to judge the precise point at which the brakes needed to be applied and there was a further comic moment as the driver, still bleeding from his wound and, not surprisingly, somewhat dazed by events, took three attempts to stop the train precisely at the point Bruce had ordered. After its final manoeuvre Bruce and the remaining members of the gang emerged and began the assault on the HVP coach which, as expected, was locked on the inside. The repeated hackings of crowbars and pick-axes made short work of the elementary locks and the gang poured into the coach, to the terror of the sorters who were frozen to the spot, their brains in a state of suspended animation.

'We'd like to buy half a dozen stamps and two premium bonds, please,' quipped Buster, as if he had spent five minutes queuing at a regular post office.

It required only one man with a pick-axe to keep the six sorters cowering in the corner as the men started work on removing the 128 mailbags. Harry slashed open the top bag to be sure that it contained the cash they wanted. It was packed tight with bundles of banknotes. Under the balaclava Harry permitted himself a slight smile. 'This is it. Let's go.'

The men formed themselves instantly into a disciplined line that enabled them to transfer the bags from the coach down the embankment and onto the lorry. The line was still long and the bags were heavy so the work was as slow as Bruce had anticipated. He had set himself a total limit of thirty minutes from the moment the train had been brought to a halt at Sears Crossing to the time he planned to be roaring away in convoy back towards Leatherslade Farm.

After twenty-nine and a half minutes Bruce called out, 'Right. Stop now! That's it.'

The men in the HVP coach demurred, pointing to

the remaining eight mail bags. Bruce's voice increased in intensity. 'I said now! Let's move!'

Thinking of the remaining thousands, the men nevertheless jumped down obediently and ran with the others towards the Landrovers and the army truck. Within seconds the convoy was off and moving. The huge diesel lay with its two attendant coaches like a beached whale, unable to come to terms with the violation it had just experienced. Meanwhile three-quarters of a mile up the track the rest of the Royal Mail and its sorting officers were wondering what had become of the engine and their colleagues.

As the convoy sped through the sleepy Buckinghamshire villages in the half light of the dawn on Thursday 8 August there were four men who were perched on top of 120 mailbags stuffed with money. They were listening to a short-wave radio which was kept permanently tuned to the police network. As the routine calls came in about checks on the security of outlying property or malfunctioning traffic lights in the centre of Leighton Buzzard the men paid scarcely more interest than that accorded to the incidents by the bored police themselves. However, as soon as a new voice came on the line, quivering with amazement, their interest perked up.

'Sarge . . .'

'Yeh? what is it?'

'You're not going to believe this, Sarge, but someone's just stolen a train.'

Only half a dozen cows swishing their tails in their vain attempt to ward off the persecuting flies, heard the trailing cheers.

CHAPTER SIX

The convoy swung off the main road from Oakley to Brill and bounced up the track to Leatherslade Farm. It was just after 4.10 am. They had left the farm less than four hours previously. They were now richer by an amount that would afford them great pleasure to determine.

As the convoy screeched to a halt the men quickly formed themselves into the same disciplined line that this time led from the truck to the farmhouse kitchen. Two of the men from George's firm took responsibility for making sure that the Landrovers and truck were under cover in case the police used helicopters to look for them.

The first sack was slashed open and its contents poured over the kitchen table. To the accompaniment of huge cheers from the excited men, the jumble of assorted five-pound, one-pound and ten-shilling notes was estimated at more than £20,000. They looked at the remaining 119 sacks and wished they had paid more attention at school when mental arithmetic had been taught.

Bruce eventually imposed a system on what threatened to become a free-for-all. Some of the more exhausted men went upstairs to collapse onto their airbeds while the counting started below. George and Buster, one from each firm, were appointed to begin the mammoth task of accurately counting the haul. It soon became possible to shorten the process when it was realized that the five-pound notes were all contained in bundles of £2500, the pounds in packets of

£500 and the ten-shilling notes in bundles of £250. As the piles took shape it became necessary to have the various denominations on different tables. Even then the sheer magnitude of the haul amazed the men.

'Look at it! It's gonna touch the ceiling,' exclaimed one of them.

'What a bleedin' birthday! What a bleedin' birthday!' Harry said to himself over and over again.

Someone else took up the refrain. 'It's Harry's birthday!'

A cigar was jammed into his mouth and lit by Buster with a wedge of Scottish and Irish banknotes which he had dangled into the flame from the cooker. Buster began to shake out the flames when a thought occurred to him.

'Anyone want this lot?'

Nobody did so Buster tossed the burning notes into the sink where they gradually shrivelled and died.

When the euphoria began to die down, Bruce and another member of George's firm took over the counting. The final total as agreed by both sides was £2,600,000, less the Scottish and Irish banknotes which nobody appeared to want. From the total were then subtracted the various 'drinks', flat fees already agreed as payable to people who had facilitated the robbery but who were not considered principal movers and who therefore would not share in the general good fortune. For each fully-accredited member of the exercise a sack was then laid out and filled with £150,000 in used and therefore untraceable banknotes. Some of the men transferred their share immediately into suitcases and other bags brought for the purpose. Others curled up with their sacks on their air-beds, finding enormous warmth and comfort from the rough sacking.

With the task of counting the money now completed, all the men grabbed the opportunity for desperately-needed sleep. They had been awake for more than twenty-four hours, in which time they had pulled off the biggest-ever raid from a train. They had all lost weight in anxiety and nervous strain and many of them found that their gloves, which they were supposed to wear at all times, had shrunk to half their regular size because their hands had sweated constantly. Only Bruce, armed with the radio, remained awake. He sat upstairs and listened to the frequent news reports and for all his lack of sleep he had never felt so alive.

It took an hour and a half for the alarm to be raised. The guard on the mail train eventually climbed onto the track to discover the cause of the delay, only to find that the engine was missing. He eventually found it, six terrified sorters, a trussed fireman and a bleeding, groaning train-driver at Bridego Bridge. The robbers were already safely inside Leatherslade Farm before details of the raid reached Scotland Yard.

Detective Inspector Fewtrell of the Buckinghamshire CID headed the investigation initially, although it was immediately apparent that the scale of the robbery left no room for doubt that he would need the additional support of Scotland Yard. The only clue they had to work on was the final threat from the robbers to the sorters as they raced away: 'Don't move for half an hour.' The police gambled on the fact that this meant that the robbers felt they would be safe thirty miles from the scene of the crime. It was unlikely they could have raced back to London which was nearly forty miles away without encountering traffic or a police patrol car within half an hour and the conclusion therefore was that they were in hiding within a thirty-mile radius of Bridego Bridge. It wasn't much to go on but it was a start and it was hoped that if they released this information it might flush the men out of their hiding-place.

The newspapers, radio and television were in an uproar. Coming so soon after the dramatic dénouement of the Stephen Ward trial, it seemed in the summer of 1963 that the very structure of British society was disintegrating in front of them. The journalists were having such a good time observing the discomfiture of the traditional ruling classes that this latest flouting of authority was seen as another piece of socially progressive news rather than a crime that struck at the heart of accepted standards of behaviour. It elevated the robbers to mythical status.

It all came as an enormous surprise to June who picked up the paper in her mother's flat and realized instantly where Buster had been the previous night and why he had been so preoccupied the past couple of months. Unlike her husband she viewed the successful outcome of the robbery with alarm and despondency. The very scale of the enterprise and the public reaction meant that the heat would never be off. If Buster were identified as one of the robbers she knew the police would never rest until he was behind bars. So much for Buster and his dreams of being so rich that they would be able to do anything they liked. So much for her dreams of family security, she thought bitterly.

Mrs Barker was in the kitchen cooking a small rasher of bacon for Nicky when June entered with the *Daily Mirror*. She sat down abruptly, devouring every detail of the front-page description of the robbery.

'You seen about that robbery, then?' chattered her mother. 'Some cheek, eh? Takes a bit of nerve, though. Still, a million quid. Here, you can feed her.'

June took the proffered plate with the small piece of bacon on it and began to cut it up and feed it to Nicky as her mother picked up the newspaper.

'Biggest ever robbery made from a train, it says here. Blimey, what I could do with a million quid! Dream come true, that is.' Mrs Barker started, recognizing the words she had just used. The implications were instantly apparent to her. 'Oh, June, no! You don't think he's on this one?'

'Dream come true, Mum. You said it yourself,' said June miserably, spearing a piece of greasy bacon.

Back at Leatherslade Farm the newspapers were being eagerly devoured as the men sat round in a circle reading the various reports of their exploits. Buster sat with his head buried in the *Daily Telegraph*. It wasn't a paper that would normally engage his interest but now he was totally captivated. 'This one says it was thirty masked men. How many in the *Express*, Ronnie?'

'Thirty in this one, too.'

'Well, if I was one of them bastards on the train I'd think there was thirty of us too,' chortled Harry.

'*Telegraph*'s got a good report. Everyone read it?' asked Buster.

'They all say a million quid. I wonder if they'll ever admit how much we really nicked?' Bruce couldn't help remembering the extraordinary silence in the farmhouse kitchen when the final total was announced. There was a full five seconds of amazed silence before the first cheer started. Even then the reaction didn't have quite the exuberance of the initial celebration when the contents of the first sack spilled over the kitchen table. Even though they had been acting under the belief that the Ulsterman's information of five million pounds on board was correct, the sheer expanse of over two and a half million pounds in banknotes was very sobering.

Buster worked out the price of one per cent of the haul which was the usual reward system.

'If they're offering ten grand now they'll have to up it to twenty-five thousand quid.'

'That'll set a few tongues wagging,' said Harry, ever the cynic.

'Not here, it won't,' rejoined Bruce sharply.

George meanwhile had found the one piece of information Fewtrell and the police had inserted for the robbers.

'Hello. Feller here says Old Bill thinks we're within a thirty-mile radius of the train.'

There was a pause while everyone digested the implications of such a statement. For a start it clearly meant that the police had not assumed that the robbers were safely back in London which had first started Bruce and Buster thinking. They all wondered whether the police were bluffing or perhaps knew even more than this one bald statement suggested.

'He's bluffing', said Buster with his usual cheeriness. 'They ain't got nothing to go on.'

Outside the farm all was peaceful. The rural Buckinghamshire countryside beauty was invaded only by the sound of distant threshing machines as harvesting continued unabated. Old Walter, aware of his miserable failure the previous night, redoubled his attempts to be helpful by acting as tea-boy.

About fifty yards from the farmhouse was the hole Buster and Harry had started to dig for burying the shredded mailbags. They had tried burning them but for some reason they seemed to be fire resistant. Instead of the mailbags crumbling instantly into ashes as they had hoped, Buster and Harry had watched with mounting alarm as they simply gave off an unpleasant black smoke that was unnecessarily ostentatious.

Walter approached the two men carefully. It was on his mind to explain that he had done the right thing the previous night but that they hadn't given him the time to get the vacuum. The driver had done precisely the same thing in order to get the train moving and they had waited for him all right. Walter felt they had cast a slur on his professional pride. All right, he had only ever driven trains in a shunting yard but presumably Ronnie Biggs had told them that and yet they had still wanted him on the job. Maybe now, after the mission had been successfully completed, he could explain and be forgiven. They weren't such bad chaps really. He admired their bravado and wished they would accept him as one of their number.

'Here you are, boys, a nice cuppa tea.'

Buster and Harry, stripped to the waist in the unaccustomed August sun, snatched the cups gratefully. Walter mistook their haste for further aggression and his gaze went to the hole they were digging. It was about six or seven feet long and about three feet wide: just the right size for a coffin. Suddenly Walter saw it all with dreadful clarity. These men who had just planned and executed the biggest robbery in the history of British crime were no juvenile delinquents. He had seen what they had done to the recalcitrant driver the previous night. They were going to kill him and bury his body here in the garden. It might be years before the bones were discovered. Walter fled back into the house. Buster and Harry looked at each other, shrugged, drained their mugs and went back to work.

Thirty seconds later an agitated Walter re-emerged from the farmhouse, dragging a reluctant Ronnie Biggs with him.

'See? See?,' cried the terrified Walter, pointing at the hole. 'I told you.'

'Nah. It's just a hole, Walter,' said Ronnie calmingly.

'It's them – they hate me. They're going to do for me. I know they are.' Walter wouldn't be comforted.

'Buster, Walter's a bit frightened,' explained Ronnie.

'Oh, yeh? Why's that, then?'

Ronnie looked embarrassed. 'He thinks you're digging his grave.'

Buster and Harry burst out laughing. Walter anxiously examined their faces before finally reassuring himself that, just as Ronnie suggested, he had imagined the whole thing. Tentatively at first, then with increasing hysteria, Walter joined in the general laughter. As soon as he saw this, Buster stopped abruptly and looked very serious.

'He's right. That's just what we *are* doing.'

The six o'clock news on the radio brought added alarm. It was now believed that army vehicles had been used in the robbery. This meant that the Landrovers and truck could no longer be used as planned in the evacuation from the farm. Bruce could sense the dismay this news caused.

Occasionally someone was seen not wearing gloves. Ronnie Biggs started to shake a bottle of tomato ketchup onto his portion of chips without wearing gloves. Bruce quickly seized Ronnie by the scruff of the neck and banged his forehead on the bottle to indicate the trace of fingerprints. Sheepishly Ronnie wiped the bottle clean.

Each successive news broadcast seemed to bring further alarms. The scale of the manhunt was clearly on an unprecedented scale, as more and more police officers from neighbouring forces were drafted in to help the Buckinghamshire police and the Scotland Yard Robbery Squad. The search for the hideout was soon intensified to include checks on all farms and outlying property. It was only a matter of time before they found Leatherslade Farm. Bruce's plan which had seemed so perfect, so simple, in theory now looked like it could be the cause of their downfall. Sitting on £2,600,000, it would be stupidity of the very highest class to be caught without having the chance to enjoy at least some of their 'earnings'.

The game of Monopoly was played that night with real money, an interesting variation devised by Buster, but the novelty soon wore off and Bruce became increasingly aware that the atmosphere of disciplined professionalism which had held things together so far was likely to disintegrate before his eyes.

George precipitated the final crisis. He felt an obligation to his men that did not include sitting patiently in an Oxfordshire farmhouse, now looking increasingly uninhabitable beneath its pile of dirty plates, empty bottles and stubbed out cigarettes, while the police got ever closer to them. 'I ain't staying. I made plans. I'm going to see a mate in Oxford.'

Buster looked anxiously at Bruce to see how he would restore control.

'This is stupid. There's no point sitting on our arses while they come and find us.'

'It was your plan, Bruce,' pointed out George maliciously.

'I know that. That's why I'm changing it. I'll get Fairclough to arrange for the dustman to come in and make sure the place is clean.'

'I don't trust that little turd,' said Harry sourly.

'You don't trust no-one, do you, Harry?' observed Ronnie Biggs.

'Not with little shits around like you.'

Ronnie took offence at the gratuitous insult. 'You can't talk to me like that. Tell him, Bruce. Tell him he can't talk to me like that.'

'Fuck off, you little shit,' said Bruce, his mind occupied with weightier matters.

'I still think we should wait till Sunday,' Buster argued. 'If we move now one of us'll get picked up.'

Everyone's thoughts ran to old Walter who was still in the kitchen making yet another round of teas. Ronnie still felt the need to defend him so when Buster argued that he would be the first one to get picked up and the first one to spill everything, Ronnie leapt in.

'Leave him alone, Buster. Old Bill don't know nothing about him.'

'They won't if we stick him six feet under,' growled Harry.

Walter chose this precise moment to emerge from the kitchen wobbling unsteadily under the influence of a tray holding fifteen mugs of steaming tea.

'Hello, boys,' he said with an attempt at the sort of cheer he wasn't feeling. 'Everything all right?'

It was just what Bruce needed to reassert control. 'I think we should take the risk. Anyone, and I mean *anyone*, Grandpa, that gets picked up, you don't know nothing. Right?'

There was a chorus of assent and a strange lightening of the general mood as the men faced action and danger again instead of the interminable passive waiting. They got to their feet and began to prepare to leave the farm under cover of darkness.

'Let's burn the place down before we go,' suggested Harry, his thirst for destruction never slaked.

'Leave it, Harry. Fairclough'll get it cleaned up. That's what we're paying him for. Fire like that'll only draw attention to the place and we can't be sure what they'll find when they put the fire out.'

'Fuck all if we do it properly,' charged Harry, but he appreciated the soundness of Bruce's argument.

All the men commenced their final preparations except Walter who was still wrestling with Bruce's final warning which had been delivered straight at him.

'Picked up?' he wondered aloud. 'What's he mean "picked up"?'

CHAPTER SEVEN

Buster was in a particularly jovial mood as he drove into the courtyard of the block of flats where June and Nicky were waiting for him. The popular morning newspapers lay on the front seat next to him. They were still full of the 'Crime of the Century' with detailed reports on the daring hold-up at Sears Crossing and the testimony of the 'witnesses'. A certain amount of alarm was expressed by the editorials which dwelled on the injuries sustained by the train driver, but Buster felt this was the only weapon left in the armory of the Establishment.

Beyond his wildest dreams was the fact that Buster and the others were being seen as modern day Robin Hoods. The thought tickled him enormously – until he remembered that Robin Hood was supposed to have redistributed his wealth. Yet indisputably the British public was on the side of the thieves. They were delighted that such a daring scheme had robbed the banks of so much money. After all, who cared about the banks?

June shared none of these thoughts. When Buster rang the bell and Nicky flew into his arms he twirled her round in the air above his head while his wife looked on stony-faced. Buster tried to embrace her but she was stiff and he only succeeded in banging her on the nose as she averted her face. He returned his attention to Nicky. 'What d'you think of your clever old man, then?' he asked gaily, although the question was really directed at June. Nicky giggled and had an attack of hiccoughs which brought her down to earth quickly.

June's mother appeared from the kitchen, wiping her hands on a tea-towel. Her face was equally gloomy. 'Law's going to come after you real hard, son.'

Buster dismissed the idea airily. 'Law ain't gonna be no trouble. I got the whole thing planned.'

'Planned is it? Like June's pregnancy?'

Buster failed to intercept the look that passed briefly between mother and daughter. His head was still myopically full of his own triumphs and the vistas of pleasure that lay before them. 'Ain't no one going to touch us now, Mum. We got it made. We're going to see the world, me and June and Nicky. Heat'll be off in a few weeks, you just wait and see.'

But Mrs Baker was not to be comforted by Buster's blandishments even if they were now backed, for the first time, by hard cash. 'You're riding for quite a fall, Buster Edwards. I just don't want you taking my daughter and my grandchild with you when it happens.'

Buster was briefly very angry. What was it with these women? They demanded things so you stole them, then when you'd stolen them they complained because either they didn't want them or they thought the emotional price to be paid was too high. 'Maybe they'd have been better off if June had married a shop-keeper or a bank clerk,' he thought and then dismissed it instantly from his mind as he caught sight of his wife's drawn and worried face. A great wave of love for her swept over him. It might have been mistaken for lust considering the effects the pregnancy had had on their sex life recently, but Buster recognized that the deep feelings of tenderness he had always held for June were the dominant emotion.

But Buster wasn't there to argue with his mother-in-law. He picked up June's already-packed suitcase and, carrying Nicky in his other arm, he walked them towards the car. June watched as Buster raised the boot and stowed her case next to some fishing tackle, a new plastic bucket and spade and three suitcases. Buster caught June's look of concern as she stared at the suitcases; she knew instinctively that they contained Buster's share of the robbery. Stiffly she walked round to the passenger door and climbed in.

'Want a nice holiday then, poppet?' Buster asked Nicky cheerily.

'Yeh. Where we going, Daddy?' the little girl demanded.

'Shepperton.'

'Is that the seaside, Daddy?'

'No, poppet. It's near the sea. That's why I bought you a new bucket and spade.'

Buster looked at June. 'It's a nice little semi. You'll like it there. Well away from our usual haunts. Give us a chance to find something really remote – just in case it gets a bit hot for us.'

For a moment June said nothing but continued to stare straight ahead, through the windscreen. Then she turned to her husband, her voice trembling. 'Buster.'

'What?'

'I've got something to tell you.'

The tone of her voice caused Buster to look at her sharply. Instinctively, telepathically, he knew what she was about to say. He pulled over to the side of the street and turned off the engine. He glanced, for the first time, at her stomach.

'You've lost it?'

June nodded.

'When?'

'Two nights ago. The doctor came. We tried to save it . . .'

This time there was no control. Waves of sobbing, like the labour contractions she would now never feel, racked her body. Buster put his arms round her and held her close as the spasms shook her. He kissed her neck gently.

'It doesn't matter. There'll be more. We've plenty of time. I love you.'

The phrases slipped out, trite, hackneyed, platitudinous and untrue. It didn't matter. It was what she needed to hear. They stayed like that for two minutes while Nicky stirred restlessly in the back seat, but, intuitively aware that this was a special moment, she didn't seek to break it. Eventually June disengaged herself and started rummaging in her handbag for a handkerchief. Buster turned on the ignition and set off for Shepperton.

Their road in Shepperton was the very model of the sort of housing that Buster affected to hate – and that went double for the middle classes who lived in them. The husbands were mostly on the lower and middle rungs of management, frequently working-class kids who had worked hard, got their 'O' Levels and training diplomas, kept their noses clean and were now the proud possessors of three-bedroom semi-detached houses with 80-foot gardens in the rear and mortgages that would keep them firmly in those jobs and gardens for the rest of their working lives.

The wives were the female equivalent – working-class girls who had left school with few qualifications but an eye for an eligible male which would do credit to an impoverished parent of the land-owning classes looking to offload his marriageable daughters. They were quick to give up their secretarial jobs and exchange the manual typewriter for the portable pushchair. It was an atmosphere of apparent family solidity and upwardly mobile professional striving that June found strangely attractive.

Settling in that night, Buster found his mind straying involuntarily to Leatherslade Farm and the things which had been left behind. As they were making the bed together June suddenly became aware that there was something missing. 'Buster, where's that other blanket? That grey one I gave you.'

'Ain't you brought it?' asked Buster, as the mental image of the grey blanket hanging over the window at Leatherslade Farm to secure the blackout grew ever larger.

The following morning, while Buster and June slept the sleep of contented lovers, the man from the neighbouring land walked his herd for milking through the field that ran parallel to Leatherslade Farm. He looked idly, then more closely at the garden by the farmhouse. Then he climbed over the fence and pushed his way through the hedge. He saw the evidence of a freshly-dug mound of earth. This marked the spot where Buster and Harry had been supposedly digging Walter's 'grave'. He was puzzled to discover that the signs of activity recently displayed by the 'decorators' were no longer evident. He looked with interest at June's grey blanket, hanging inside the farm-house living-room window. In the shed he found a five-ton army truck with its bonnet covered in yellow paint as if someone had been trying to disguise its origins. He remembered dimly the television news he had seen the previous night. Weren't the Great Train Robbers supposed to have used army vehicles to carry the money from the train to the hideout? He went back to his own farmhouse and rang the police at Aylesbury.

True to the staunch traditions of the British constabulary, the police at Aylesbury completely ignored the information. At the time they were engaged in a massive search of properties within a thirty-mile radius of Sears Crossing but had not yet approached the villages of Brill or Oakley, between which Leather-slade Farm was to be found. In any case approximately a further 399 telephone calls were logged at the police station at Aylesbury, all offering similar clues or sightings of the robbers.

The following morning the farmer telephoned again and this time the message reached the outlying police station in the nearby village of Waddesdon. A sergeant and constable set out to investigate and found matters at the farm much as relayed to them. Their suspicions aroused by the army lorry, they forced open the door of the locked garage and found the two Landrovers which made up the rest of the convoy that had transported the money from the train.

Outside the Old Bailey, Buster, Bruce and Harry waited in the unseasonal damp for the emergence of Fairclough from the Central Criminal Court. Fairclough was their very own bent lawyer whose aspirations to ape the living standards of his fellow, but more successful, barristers had led him into the fringes of the activities favoured by some of the clients he defended. He was aware of the train robbery from early on and had made himself responsible for finding the 'dustman' – the man who would clean the hiding place of all traces of their occupation.

Fairclough eventually emerged in wig and gown and set off in the direction of his chambers. The three thieves struggled to keep abreast.

'Sorry to keep you waiting, boys. Jury's only just retired,' explained Fairclough to nobody in particular, his eyes set dead ahead.

'You're a smug little prick, ain't you?' spat Buster venomously. The three of them were all spitting with rage but were in no position to display their hostility openly.

'Why ain't you been ringing us back?' asked Bruce, although all three of them were fairly sure they knew the answer.

'I wanted to be quite sure my friend had done his work at the farm.'

'And has he?'

Fairclough favoured them with a direct look for the first time. 'Not as yet, no,' he replied evenly.

Harry lost his scarcely concealed temper. 'You fucker. I'll do you,' and he tried to get past Bruce to attack the lawyer. Bruce and Buster both applied the necessary muscle to prevent the outbreak of such an unseemly fracas.

Fairclough smiled thinly. 'No need for undue alarm, my friends. He'll be there this afternoon. Tomorrow at the latest. Your little change of plan has caused major adjustments, you know.'

Bruce felt a cold stab of fear. The police were getting ever nearer. By the following day they might have found Leatherslade Farm and nobody knew how much incriminating evidence they had unwittingly left behind.

'You've let us down, you bastard,' he groaned.

Fairclough seemed amused. 'You haven't been careless with your prints, have you?' he asked with seeming innocence.

'We'd better get back there now,' Bruce stated, looking at the others.

'Yeh. We can burn the bleeder down,' agreed Harry, who hadn't lost his vision of a major conflagration.

'I think I left my trousers there,' complained Buster as the three of them left Fairclough striding towards the Inner Temple while they made their way back to Bruce's Jaguar.

An hour later they were speeding west on the A40 past High Wycombe listening to the Test Match Special Service of the BBC giving ball by ball commentary of the final test match between England and the West Indies. None of the men were particularly interested in the cricket, despite the praise that was being lavished on the Yorkshire batsman Philip Sharpe as he made his second half century of the match in a vain effort to prevent the West Indies winning the match by eight wickets and the series by three games to one. It was simply that the bucolic voice of John Arlott was the perfect background to their individual thoughts as they stared out through the windows of the car at the English countryside in full bloom.

On the fall of Jim Parks's wicket, trapped lbw by Charlie Griffith for twenty-three from the ball that the England batsmen were convinced was not a legitimate delivery, they all seemed to rejoin the commentry at the same time to hear the enthusiastic tones of Brian Johnston handing back to Broadcasting House for the lunchtime news. The leading item stunned them as the newsreader in the traditional measured tones of the BBC stated calmly, 'Police investigating the Great Train Robbery in which thieves made off with more than two-and-a-half million pounds have just announced that they have found what they believe to be the robbers' hideout. It is Leatherslade Farm near the village of Oakley in Buckinghamshire. Detective Superintendent Fewtrell, Head of the Buckinghamshire CID, said this afternoon, "The place is one big clue".'

Bruce's hand reached forward and snapped off the radio. Although they had known for a couple of days that there was a strong possibility that the police might find the farm before all trace of their occupation had been destroyed, the bald statement of the discovery shocked them. Buster was the one to articulate their innermost feelings.

'That's it,' he said quietly. 'We're nicked.'

In a transport café in Ruislip the three shell-shocked men sat mournfully stirring their cups of thick brown tea. Even Buster's habitual cheerfulness was missing.

Bruce tried hard to rally his troops. 'Come on, you two. They won't find nothing to connect us to it anyway.'

It didn't seem to have the desired effect. He tried another tack. 'We've all got safe houses arranged, ain't we?'

The words of the chief investigating officer, as relayed by the BBC, seemed to swim around in their heads. ' "The place is one big clue". What the hell does that mean?' wondered Harry.

'Prints, probably.'

Harry felt his professional competence was in question. 'We was wearing gloves, weren't we?' he stated categorically. A guilty silence ensued as the men recalled the times that they weren't.

'We should go and burn the bleeder down,' he reiterated.

Bruce looked at him with intense irritation, unaware that this had simply become Harry's reflex violent response to every setback. 'Don't be crazy. The place'll be swarming with the Law.'

'And journalists,' added Buster. 'Don't forget we're famous now. We're bigger than Christine Keeler or the Beatles.'

The thought of Bruce and himself arriving in New York or Hollywood with their wives, being sped through the city from the airport to a luxury hotel in a large black limousine, floated irresistibly through

Buster's mind. When he got out of the limousine it was only to look up at the forbidding façade of Worm-wood Scrubs. He returned to reality.

The others didn't sound as though they welcomed the prospect of impending fame, even of the notorious kind.

'Oh, great,' said Harry gloomily. 'That's all we need.'

'It'll just make everyone keen to be the one that fingers us,' pointed out Bruce.

'And there's that fucking reward,' Harry added.

The three of them were transfixed by the prospect of having pulled off the crime of the century, sitting on £150,000 each and being unable to spend it.

The waitress dropped a bill for one and sixpence onto the table. Buster started to pat his empty pockets. 'Anyone got two bob for the bill?'

CHAPTER EIGHT

The discovery of Leatherslade Farm produced results all right – but not those that had been expected on all sides. Among the objects which the police examined were a Monopoly board, a dropped knife and some discarded wrappers from the bundles of banknotes. Many of the robbers were identified from the finger-prints found on these articles, but then the unpredictable nature of the British public manifested itself.

For the same reason that made them cheer the underdog they decided that they didn't want the police to catch the Great Train Robbers. The forces of law and order were horrified. 1963 had been a bad year. First there was that crippling big freeze, then the awful Profumo scandal which nearly brought down Macmillan's Government. The Prime Minister, in ill health anyway and with no obvious young successor in a demoralized Conservative Party, was pictured in the papers shooting grouse on the moors of Scotland while his capital city was overrun with rumours of an extraordinary kind – ranging from stories of whipping parties in Mayfair society houses, in which featured a man in a leather mask who was supposedly a cabinet minister, to the notion that eight members of the High Court had been discovered in Richmond Park engaging in dubious practices with ladies of ill repute. The Prime Minister with his mordant wit was reported to have responded that he could well imagine two judges in such a compromising position but eight seemed far-fetched.

At the end of July Stephen Ward killed himself

rather than face the jail sentence that was being cooked up for him on the last day of his trial. It was clear to many people in Britain that the savage manner in which Ward was treated was in some measure the result of the Establishment's desire to regain some of its lost credibility. A new technologically-based Labour Party, led by Harold Wilson who paid more attention to electoral strategy and public relations than the old party issues of nationalization and disarmament in Clause Four seemed to be racing ahead in the opinion polls. Macmillan, the Tory Party and the very ruling class they had represented for 120 years, since the age of Robert Peel and the Great Reform Bill, seemed doomed to vanish with the same certainty that the dinosaur vanished from the face of the earth.

It was in this atmosphere of a fevered nation, beset by political and social disorder, that the Great Train Robbery took place. It accounted for the ferocity with which the robbers were pursued and for the public response which was to cheer them on from the sidelines even though each day brought news of new arrests.

George was picked up in Oxford, where he had rented a room as soon as he had left Leatherslade Farm. Ronnie Biggs was picked up a week later and by the middle of September ten people were either 'helping police with their enquiries' or else under arrest for robbery. The big fear had always been that Old Walter would be identified, but in some crazy fashion, just as he had bumbled his way through the operation itself, he managed to bumble his way through the roundup. The police never got a sniff of Old Walter.

At this point the trail went cold and the Establishment, which had looked forward to a spectacular show trial wherein it could demonstrate to the lawless and the electorate alike that its authority could not be flouted with impunity, became anxious that the opportunity would be denied it. It was in just such an atmosphere that Richard Poyser, Assistant Commissioner of the Metropolitan Police, was summoned to a meeting with Sir James McDowell, Minister of State at the Home Office in the latter's West End club in Pall Mall.

They met in the smoking-room after the Minister had emerged replete but not noticeably well tempered after dining with a journalist who had friends in influential places and who persistently wrote about the Chief Enaharo affair, to the irritation of McDowell's superior, the Home Secretary.

'Ah, Poyser,' began McDowell as the policeman stumbled awkwardly to his feet. 'Don't get up. Drink?'

'No, thank you, sir.' Poyser declined, hoping his abstemiousness might help defuse what was clearly a highly inflammable situation. Unfortunately McDowell was unimpressed.

'Another whisky and soda, George,' he ordered summoning a grizzled club retainer. He turned to Poyser. 'You can't go around consuming orange juice with such evident martyrdom. It does nothing for your credibility or that of the police force.'

'Sorry, sir,' apologized Poyser tightly. 'I just don't drink on duty.' It was an opening the experienced politician was not going to ignore.

'Since conventional police tactics do not appear to have unearthed either Reynolds or Edwards, it might conceivably help your career if you were to *start* drinking.'

Poyser blushed, accentuating his normal ruddy features. He began to offer McDowell routine assurances but he was cut short.

'This is not just another robbery with violence. It's a crime against the very structure of our society.'

Poyser began to bristle. The police had done well so far. He knew that. Why did this politician make him feel so inadequate? 'We know the men in most of the cases, sir. They've been very careless with their prints.'

McDowell was in no mood to donate Brownie points to the police force. 'All the more reason why they should be under lock and key by now. This government has barely survived the Profumo disaster. We really cannot afford for the British Government to take the side of a gang of burglars against the forces of law and justice.'

Poyser laughed. He thought that was what the Minister's sarcasm demanded. 'I hardly think that's likely, Sir James.'

Sir James took the whisky and soda from the proferred silver tray, leaned back in his armchair and looked hard at this idiot who, for reasons not apparent to him now, ranked second in the official Metropolitan Police hierarchy.

'Really, Mr Poyser? Do I take it that nobody in Scotland Yard looks at a newspaper any longer?'

Poyser felt he was now on safer ground. The banality of the popular press was an easy butt on which to re-aim the politician's wrath. 'Oh, that's just Fleet Street drivel. Nobody believes all that Robin Hood nonsense.'

McDowell saw the opening and drove home the rapier. 'Indeed? It may come as a surprise to you and your colleagues at Scotland Yard, Poyser, but the very same people who read that Fleet Street drivel, as you call it, also have the vote now. A retrogressive step, possibly, but a fact of political life, I'm afraid.'

Poyser tried to regroup. It seemed awfully hot to

him in the smoking-room. The blazing fire which had previously seemed to be largely decorative now appeared to be a veritable Dante's inferno. Poyser shifted in the deep leather upholstery and tried desperately to think of something he could offer McDowell as a hostage to fortune. 'A couple of weeks, sir. That's all it'll take. These criminals have never done anything bigger than a High Street bank before this. Ten days, tops.'

McDowell continued to stare at Poyser, unimpressed with his performance, sceptical of his ability to find either Bruce or Buster who were now considered the ringleaders. Poyser wondered how long he really had before he was moved sideways, 'kicked upstairs', or simply pensioned off. He ran his finger round the inside of his sweaty collar. His gaze wandered from McDowell's implacable stare to the circulating figure of George the waiter.

'Actually, I've changed my mind about that drink . . .' he started.

Meanwhile one of the ringleaders was quite enjoying the seclusion of his enforced stay in the anonymity of Shepperton. In the absence of June, who had taken Nicky to explore the swings and slides of the local park, Buster was watching the flat racing on television with his stockinged feet up on the coffee table and sipping beer that was not too cold. Buster could sometimes demonstrate an amazing capacity to absorb endless hours of television. He could sit through *Andy Pandy*, or *Rag, Tag and Bobtail* with Nicky, a whole afternoon with Peter O'Sullivan at Kempton Park and then whatever imported American crime series or cowboy series was available. Normally if he wasn't working he would be looking to spend large amounts of time drinking heavily in the pubs and clubs of

South London. But with the police manhunt getting ever more intense, there wasn't much incentive to re-visit his old haunts.

Buster was looking critically at a two-year-old filly by the exotic name of Bogart Hole Clough which he fancied at odds of 25–1 when the doorbell rang loudly, shattering his spiritual contentment. He swore softly under his breath, turned down the sound on the tele-vision and padded out of the lounge into the hall and the comparative safety of the dining-room which looked out over the garden.

Outside the front door a young schoolgirl had her eyes glued to the letter-box. As Buster waddled through the hall she stood up and turned to her mother. 'He's in there, Mum. I just saw him go into the dining-room.'

Her mother, pleased that her intuition had been correct and that possible male rescue was at hand, was yet disconcerted by this eccentric behaviour from her new next-door neighbour. She looked at her ten-year-old son. 'David, go round the back and knock on the window. Tell the man to answer the door.'

The little boy, socks round his ankles, schoolcap askew on his head, set off like a greyhound out of a trap. He climbed over the gate separating the front of the house from the back and arrived in the back garden at the precise time that Buster was starting to draw the dining-room curtains. The boy rapped on the window as requested. 'My mum says open the front door.'

Buster, faced with this urchin apparition, became speechless with rage and embarrassment. 'Piss off, little kid, before I do you,' he shouted, all thoughts of hiding in obscurity temporarily abandoned. His de-meanour was not noticeably improved by the seem-ingly magical appearance of the little boy's mother, smiling graciously and his sister, Amy. Buster stood transfixed as he faced his neighbours for the first time.

'Hello, you're Mr Green, aren't you?' said the woman. She waited patiently for Buster to open a window or, more reasonably, suggest they all met at the front door. Buster remained immobile. The woman was forced to continue the conversation in ludicrous fashion by shouting through the closed window.

'I'm sorry to trouble you, but I've done a very silly thing and locked myself out.'

Buster seemed unimpressed.

'Next door,' the woman explained. 'I'm Linda Simpson and these are my children – Amy's thirteen and David's ten. Say hello to Mr Green, children.'

'Hello,' chorused the children obediently.

They waited for a response. ''Allo,' said Buster ungraciously. He waited for them to go away now that the introductions had been effected, but Mrs Simpson was made of sterner stuff.

Linda paused, trying to work out how to bring the somewhat stilted conversation round to the pressing matter of getting into her own house. Middle-class etiquette prevented her asking a direct question, so she persisted with her circumlocution.

'You've got a little girl, haven't you?'

'Yeh,' said Buster reluctant to deny the fact since this sort of woman obviously spent hours with her nose pressed to the window pane.

'Nicky, isn't it?'

'Yeh. Look, was there something?' Buster was determined to resolve the situation without further debate.

Linda simpered. 'Well, I don't like to ask, but neighbours . . . you know. It's just that my husband is away on business today. In Leicester. He's a

69

Management Consultant,' she added proudly, knowing these words would inevitably produce a guaranteed reflex emotion of awe and envy in most Shepperton households. Buster seemed immune to their power though.

'You want a lift up or something?'

'Well . . . actually . . . I was thinking. . . . Have you got a ladder, Mr Green?'

Ten minutes later Buster was atop the ladder he had found in the garden shed and attempting to force open the bedroom window of the Simpson house. June, walking home contentedly from an afternoon in the warm September sunshine with Nicky, became aware that her husband was breaking and entering the house next door in full sight of all the neighbours. Her heart missed a beat and she broke into a run, charging up the street with the little girl. 'Buster,' she screamed, 'No, no!'

The smiling Linda, Amy and David emerged from behind the garden bush which had obscured them from June's sight. Linda extended her imperturbable Shepperton welcome. 'Hello, Mrs Green. This must be Nicky. Hello, Nicky! This is Amy and David.'

June remained nonplussed. Linda continued. 'Your husband has very kindly agreed to help me. You see, I locked myself out.'

June merely stood there with a silly grin on her face. Buster clucked and returned to effecting his legal entry.

An hour later June sat in front of the mirror, putting the finishing touches to her make-up. Buster was unimpressed. 'How long you going to be, then?'

'As long as it takes.'

'I don't know what's so special about her,' Buster grumbled.

'Ain't nothing special. We helped her get in the house. She's just being friendly in return.'

'Friendly? Nosy I calls it.'

'Don't be so suspicious, Buster. It'd look worse if we didn't go now. 'Sides, Nicky needs friends and them kids seem quite nice.'

'You're only going for tea. What you need to doll yourself up for?'

'It's different here, Buster. Different class of people round here.'

'Too bleedin' right,' agreed Buster bitterly.

June sat with her teacup perched carefully on her lap, admiring Linda's garden as Amy, David and Nicky played a game which appeared to involve a lot of running about and banging of bedroom doors.

'My husband loves that garden. I mean, we can't find him in the house between April and October. I mean, on weekends of course,' Linda added quickly in case June interpreted her observation as implying that Mr Simpson was periodically unemployed.

'Are most people like that round here?' asked June.

'Well, they're not like John, of course. I mean, he's an expert. But, yes, they're very proud of their gardens round here.'

The conversation was interrupted by a series of shrieks and the three children came racing through the dining-room, David's trailing leg knocking over Linda's sewing-box whose contents spilled over the floor. Linda's composure slipped for the moment.

'David, stop that!'

June smiled as she recognized the Cockney working-class vowels that Linda had paid good money to an elocution teacher to eradicate.

'Nicky! You mind what you're doing,' she called, anxious to be seen to be in tune with current trends in child-rearing in Shepperton.

She turned back to face her hostess and listen to

the passage of success from her early married days living behind a council estate in St Albans.

The following morning was a Saturday which allowed Amy and David to go on making a racket after 8.30 am when they normally left the house to go to their local schools. Linda came downstairs and picked up the morning newspaper and two unpleasant-looking letters in brown envelopes with official writing on them. She set the paper down and laid the table with place mats, cutlery, milk and cereal packets. As she waited for the kettle to boil she glanced idly at the newspaper. There, along with photographs of Bruce and Harry, was a mug-shot of Buster under the headline 'The Wanted Men'. Linda's eyes widened. She gulped and called for her husband. The kettle began to whistle with piercing shrillness as she picked up the telephone and dialled 999.

It took about twenty minutes for a dozen police cars, from, seemingly, all directions to screech to a halt outside the 'Green's' house. Linda and the children stood at the front door as the posse covered possible exits and the primary force smashed down the front door. Inspector Jack Mitchell, the new detective in charge of the hunt for the remaining train robbers, walked up the drive shouting through a megaphone.

'Ronald Edwards, the house is completely surrounded by police officers. Come out and give yourself up quietly.'

The message was repeated twice more as the neighbours gathered in their front rooms and on their porches to witness in amazement the transformation of their quiet suburban neighbourhood. The men with the axes took only a few moments to smash their way through the front door. The leading officers charged into the kitchen where they discovered evidence of recent occupation and hasty departure. The bowls of half-eaten cereal and plates of deserted toast suggested that the Edwards family had probably left in the last thirty minutes.

Mitchell entered to find the birds had flown. He walked over to the table where the newspaper had been left open at the page which had so engaged the attention of Linda Simpson. Over the photograph of himself which appeared under the caption 'The Policeman Who Leads The Chase' someone, presumably Buster himself, had drawn a comic moustache, beard and spectacles. Mitchell hurled the paper to the floor. He was not amused.

CHAPTER NINE

'Gone?' echoed Richard Poyser dully. 'What do you mean, "gone"?'

Mitchell thought hard. Was this a trick question or was the Assistant Commissioner being rhetorical? He compromised. 'We missed them by about half an hour, sir.'

Poyser turned round to face him, away from the view over the Victoria Embankment he found so seductive. His face was harsh. The pressure exerted by the Government on him and the Commissioner was starting to tell. Poyser didn't like dealing with the newspapers and the television cameras. He was an old-fashioned policeman who had started his life in the force pounding the quiet streets of Dorchester in the 1930s. He had always done things by the book, kept his nose clean, achieved his promotions in un-spectacular but merited fashion. His strength was bureaucratic administration and a quiet personal command. Somehow, in the wake of the Great Train Robbery, he had been thrust forward to receive the full force of media attention. He didn't like it.

'That is not something I can release in a Press state-ment, Mitchell, as well you know. And it's not going to do anything for the Commissioner's state of health either.' Poyser didn't see why he shouldn't make Mitchell feel as badly as he did. It helped to shovel the blame about.

'We were there within ten minutes of the phone call from the next-door neighbour.'

Poyser continued to look past him. It bothered the

Assistant Commissioner that everyone was making such a big fuss about Edwards and Reynolds. To be honest, he had been expecting a certain amount of praise to be wafted his way after capturing ten of the gang so quickly. Really, everyone was expecting an impossible success rate these days. What was it about Edwards and Reynolds that was turning them into little media stars? Poyser bemoaned the way of the world.

Mitchell took his continued silence for implied criticism. 'We reckon they've gone back to their own patch,' he explained, as extenuation. 'They'll feel better protected in South London. No villain like Edwards is going to feel secure outside London.'

'I don't want theories, Mitchell. I want these men locked up.' Poyser thought unhappily he was turning into a robot, a parrot, simply reiterating the phrases that had been used on him, making sure the next man in the line received the same sort of bollocking. Was this the summit of his ambitions in the Force?

Inevitably Mitchell had the same defence that he had used himself. 'I think you've got to be positive about things, sir. We've caught ten of the bastards already. It won't be long before they start squealing.'

Poyser's normally phlegmatic temperament started to fray at the edges. 'Come on, Inspector. You read the newspapers too. Since those pictures of Edwards and Reynolds have been released they've become proper little folk heroes.'

Jack Mitchell thought back three or four years to the time he had first come across Buster Edwards. It was in a rather sleazy Lambeth nightclub that was barely more than a room for drinking after hours, with a couple of one-arm bandits thrown in. The police kept a fairly watchful eye on it when it became apparent that it was a place for trading information about crimes past, present and future. Buster owned it, in partnership with two other villains, and though they might almost have turned it into a relatively honest living, the temptation to continue the life of action and excitement while drinking or distributing the profits from the alcohol remained too great.

Eventually the club had outlasted its usefulness for Buster. He had been involved in an armed robbery in which he had been injured. With the agreement of his partners they decided to demolish the club, claim the insurance and pretend that their injuries had been sustained while resisting a bunch of East End gangsters who were trying to screw them for protection money. Mitchell had been the first plain-clothes detective on the spot. Buster had been impressed by the speed with which Mitchell had smelled a rat but there had been nothing he could do. Nobody could prove that Buster had not received his wound in the course of a fracas at the club, and it was only to be expected that the traditional conspiracy of underworld silence would prevent Buster from naming the villains who had supposedly worked him over. Mitchell retired from the fray but he had marked Buster's card all right.

'I know Edwards, sir. I've known him for a few years now. I can get the word out this morning if you like.'

Mitchell, like most serving officers in the police force, always knew somebody who could get word to any known villain. Buster was a relatively small-time thief who had suddenly pulled off a job beyond anybody's comprehension. He would be just as concerned at the scale of the manhunt he had unleashed as the police and politicians. Mitchell thought he might welcome returning some of the money and giving himself up in return for a reduced sentence.

Not that Mitchell could guarantee the latter – but it always helped to have the police supporting the idea of a lesser charge.

Poyser wasn't biting. The heat on his back was too intense. 'No, Jack. No deal. Not on this one. I want those bastards nailed to the floor. And so do you. Your neck's on the line too.'

The threat of dismissal as the price of failure was all too clear to the ambitious Mitchell. He wasn't going to jeopardise a promising career in the Metropolitan Police for anyone – for Buster Edwards or Richard Poyser.

The search for the remaining train robbers was intensified. Information on their whereabouts was being paid for at almost any price. A tight web of security still veiled Buster and Bruce, but other, less popular members, were not so fortunate. The police called in all favours as the story resolutely refused to be moved off the front pages of the newspapers. Eventually one villain bought his freedom from arrest on a charge of breaking and entering with the news that one of the robbers was holed up in a flat in the fashionable St Johns Wood area of North London.

As had happened at Shepperton, the police arrived in disproportionately large numbers to a small row of mews houses just off the Abbey Road. The train robber, who, like the rest of the gang, had by now developed the sixth sense of a hunted animal, managed to get out of the bedroom window and onto the roof as mass pandemonium broke out down below. Arc lights, arranged for the purpose, roamed the sky like the introduction to a Hollywood film. Eventually they discovered a small figure, crouched low as it tried to keep its balance, scrampering along the terraced roofs.

The robber clambered inelegantly down the other

side of the building and dropped awkwardly the last ten feet. As he hit the ground he ran straight into the burly figures of two policemen, one of whom instantly seized him and held his hands behind his back, while fumbling at the same time for the handcuffs. The other copper simply began to punch the helpless captive in the stomach. Eventually the first policeman shone his torch into the victim's face and swore.

'Save your breath. It's not Edwards or Reynolds. It's just that racing-driver git.'

The policeman who had hit him, started hitting him again, this time in frustration rather than exuberance.

Buster observed the tightening of the net with growing alarm. He, June and Nicky had been found a place by his close friend with legitimate connections, Jimmy Phillips, a large ugly man of limited intelligence but dog-like devotion to Buster and June. He had been a boxer earlier in his life but had retired with a lifetime record of seven wins and twenty-three defeats, together with a nose which had been broken so often that it resembled nothing so much as a corkscrew. As a result he was always known as Jimmy the Nose.

After the near fiasco at Shepperton Jimmy the Nose had taken the unusual risk of hiding Buster and his family in his own house. This was a brave if foolhardy venture because the police knew of his long friendship with Buster and had already paid two fruitless if aggressive visits. If Buster had been caught in Jimmy's house, Jimmy would almost certainly have been charged as if he had been a full participating member of the gang that robbed the train rather than as an accessory after the fact, such was the hysteria still attending the manhunt.

Fortunately, after two days Jimmy had acquired the lease of a large house beside the River Thames in Wraysbury. Here the Edwards family could be perfectly safe. June wore a black wig when she went shopping in the village in case descriptions of her were ever issued and Buster remained holed up in the house, only venturing out very occasionally to meet Bruce or to conduct some other piece of urgent business which Jimmy couldn't organize on his behalf.

Such meetings now required the sort of detailed planning and split-second timing that had marked the original robbery. Jimmy arrived one night to pick him up from Wraysbury and drive twenty miles west into the outskirts of London. To avoid the possibility of being tailed Buster got quickly out of Jimmy's car and into another one parked in a pre-arranged spot in a West London street. This car drove on until it reached the boundary of Lambeth where yet another vehicle was waiting to take him into the docks area at Rotherhithe where Bruce was expecting him.

At the back of a greasy-spoon café Bruce sat half hidden by a coat stand. Both men refrained from much display of emotion at this first meeting since the great days of early August, though each man recoiled slightly at the drastically-changed appearance of the other. Bruce was wearing spectacles and a moustache while Buster's face was by now almost entirely obliterated by an impressive array of beard, moustache and side whiskers.

Each sat examining the limited, badly-scrawled menu with studied deliberation. Eventually in a tone of voice which it was impossible to overhear, Buster said, 'All right?'

'Yeh, great. You get here OK?'

'No sweat. Mind you, cost enough, didn't it?'

'A pony. How much did you pay?'

'You heard about Ray?'

Bruce raised his eyebrows – his traditional manner of making Buster feel stupid. Buster failed to react and Bruce became aware that his eyebrows were now totally invisible beneath the spectacles.

'Course I did,' he responded inadequately.

'Anyone grass?'

'It's been sorted out,' said Bruce shortly.

There was a pause while the waiter delivered two plates of unappetising fried eggs, sausages, baked beans and chips, and a chipped pot of tea. Buster smacked his lips, poured HP Sauce and tomato ketchup indiscriminately over the food, picked up his knife and fork and started to eat. Bruce winced at this display of gastronomic suicide and poured himself a cup of tea.

'What's all this I hear about you not liking Mexico?' he began accusingly.

The fork hovered near Buster's open mouth, tomato ketchup hanging from the suspended chip. 'It's not me, Bruce. It's June. She ain't sure she'll like it. She keeps talking about Australia.'

Bruce was committed to the Mexican venture and used the words that had always struck a chord with Buster. 'It's wonderful. Sun, sea, white sand, just like them travel brochures. And the tits, Buster. Just think of the tits.'

Buster thought about them. 'Oh, you can get all that in Australia. And they speak the language out there.'

He considered the last statement further. 'Well, sort of,' he amended.

Bruce didn't like this vision of Buster thinking for himself. It made him feel a trifle uneasy. 'You don't want to start messing about with Australia, Buster,' he warned. 'Full of convicts, it is. Besides,' he pointed out reasonably, 'Interpol's going to be looking there. First place they'll look, Australia.'

Buster didn't want an argument which he knew he'd lose or to get trapped into a verbal agreement with Bruce. He would then have to go home and explain to June why he had allowed Bruce to change their own plans. Sometimes he wished June and Bruce could sort things out between them and tell him afterwards what had been decided. It would be much quicker in the long run and easier on all of them.

'I just know we gotta get out of here as fast as we can but June don't want to leave London. It's been hard enough getting her to move out to Wraysbury. She's a town girl. Like me.'

Buster thought quickly. The last sentence hadn't sounded right. 'A townie, I mean,' he added quickly before Bruce could interject with the inevitable withering sarcasm.

Foiled, Bruce concentrated his attack elsewhere. 'Does she know what the Law's like at the moment? Christ, if we'd taken the bleeding Crown Jewels they couldn't be coming after us any harder.'

Buster started to squirm. 'I know that, Bruce. It's just that her mother . . .'

'Oh, for fuck's sake, Buster, I don't want to hear about June's mother. Take her with you, if you're so keen.'

'I ain't keen!' Buster was appalled at the suggestion. 'I can't stand the old dragon. Christ, I don't want her wherever we go. Prefer to be in the Scrubs.'

Bruce pushed his plate of rapidly cooling fried grease to one side and stood. He leaned over Buster and said quietly but pointedly, 'That's precisely where you'll end up unless you sort out June. You realize you can live like a king out in Mexico for a couple of grand a year?'

This was a sore point with Buster. As Bruce disappeared into the thick cigarette smoke that rose from the formica-covered tables, Buster muttered to himself, 'I hope you're right, mate. Way we're getting through our dough we'll only have enough for six months anyway.'

But Bruce was gone and nobody else seemed interested in the problems of a man with over £100,000 to spend.

Three days later another serious dent was made in the large pile of used banknotes when Jimmy arrived by river with fresh supplies of tinned food. Buster was waiting for him in the living-room with a series of bundles of banknotes all neatly sorted and labelled. After greeting June and Nicky warmly, Jimmy sat down and looked through the money displayed in front of him.

'Think you can manage?' asked Buster rhetorically.

Jimmy grinned. 'I think so. Who's this Albert Stapleton?' he queried, picking up one of the bundles labelled with an unfamiliar name.

'He's the bloke arranging the transfer to Swiss francs,' explained Buster.

Jimmy nodded. He remembered hearing something about Albert Stapleton. The name definitely rang a bell. 'Oh, yeh. I heard of him. He's a wanker.'

Buster looked upset. 'He come highly recommended.'

'He's a wanker,' repeated Jimmy decisively. 'Buster, you must be crazy letting Stapleton handle it from here. You should be in Switzerland yourself. It's the only way you can be sure you ain't bein' taken for a ride.'

Buster was amused. 'Taken for a ride? Jesus Christ, I ain't been outside this house in six months. 'Part from when I sees Bruce. You know that. Who's the Prime Minister these days?'

Jimmy ignored the jibe and pointed at the money. 'Tell me about this lot.'

Buster handed over the largest wad containing £3,000 in used five and one pound notes. 'This one's yours. This is for Keith. He's looking for a place abroad for us. Which reminds me. What's the news on the passports?'

Jimmy looked embarrassed. This was the one area where he - was having particular trouble helping Buster. 'Very difficult, Buster. None of the regular forgers'll touch it. They've all been turned over by the Law. I'm having to go to some highly dodgy sources.'

Jimmy picked up the next pile and made a face. 'Here! What's this lot for? It's foreign.' He didn't like the look of the Scottish and Irish notes and wondered if any had been slipped into his own share. An unpleasant aroma wafted from them. He sniffed. 'And it pongs.'

'No point having June wash and iron it. It's only for Fairclough. He's got the lot in ten-bob notes.'

'Poor old Fairclough,' mused Jimmy. 'Why don't nobody like him?'

''Cause he's a two-faced prick,' answered Buster shortly.

Jimmy considered this crushing indictment. 'Maybe. But he knows enough to put the lot of you inside.'

It was true enough. Fairclough might be a useful contact when things were going well but he was vain, greedy and ambitious, like the thieves. As each new arrest was made and announced Fairclough started to worry that one of the thieves was going to identify him. He started to think of ways in which he could explain his connection with them while at the same time denying all knowledge of the train job. Contact had been made when he had defended Harry on a charge two years before and gained a verdict of 'Not Guilty' even though Harry had already confessed his guilt to Fairclough. Harry was the contact. As long as Harry was free Fairclough felt relatively secure. And as long as the police didn't finger Fairclough, Buster and Bruce thought they had the time to get out of the country.

Two days after Jimmy had collected the money from Buster to distribute, half a dozen police mounted the stairs of a sleazy Soho apartment building and hacked down the door of the room where Harry was hiding.

CHAPTER TEN

Harry Stenford's greatest virtue was his loyalty. It was ironic, therefore, that it was his loyalty that proved to be his downfall. A harsher critic might have pointed out that loyalty in such a man was simply a derivative of the stupidity that Harry also manifested with some consistency. Being too stupid to think for himself, he was easily convinced by the smooth-talking Bruce and the even faster-talking Buster. Harry, of course, was also tremendously strong and had proved his worth on a number of occasions in the past.

True to his essentially generous nature Harry was determined that his success at Bridego Bridge should benefit people other than himself. One of those recipients of his fortune was Sally, a forty-five-year-old whore who had seen better days. Harry liked going to prostitutes to slake his sexual thirst. They didn't ask him to talk to them in the off-putting manner of the non-professional women who had interested him sexually. Once the price was negotiated he had only to look forward to his own pleasure. It was an eminently satisfactory relationship.

Unfortunately he soon found that the fast turnover of prostitutes and their rooms of engagement was confusing. No sooner had he found a woman who appeared to understand his needs than she was replaced by some evil-smelling foreign girl. Harry wasn't at all happy when this happened. His natural xenophobia was intensified.

However he could always rely on Sally. Sally

seemed to be an independent by nature and managed to retain possession of the same room for years on end. Harry could always find her. After the first two or three years of physical intimacy Harry had developed the habit of talking to *her* while he was dressing. He found that she had a thirteen-year-old son who had been born deaf and most of her earnings went to pay for the boy's residence at a special school in the country. Harry liked hearing about the little boy and his progress. It gave him a feeling of family-once-removed. He also liked the fact that Sally wore a purple nightdress in bed. It reminded him a bit of his own mother. After three or four years of intermittent intercourse Harry also discovered that he no longer gained any tangible sexual pleasure from their relationship, but by this time he was so intimately involved with Sally as a person that he couldn't even contemplate the prospect of no longer seeing her. In addition he found out that her other clients were no longer finding with Sally the supreme erotic experience and she was actually becoming dependent on Harry's weekly visit.

Despite receiving information that the police were looking for him, Harry took a calculated risk in seeing Sally while the hunt was on. She needed the money more than he wanted the sex but he needed the human meeting even more than she needed the money so he sneaked into Soho to see her. Poyser and Mitchell in their methodical way had covered every regular contact of every Train Robbery suspect. When Harry darted up the stairs of Sally's Old Compton Street flat a call went to the Yard.

The sound of a dozen uniformed Metropolitan policemen tramping up two flights of stairs was unmistakable even to Harry and Sally at the height of their romantic ardour. There was no way out of

Sally's room and it was too much to expect even the British police not to look in the wardrobe. Sally dived for spectacles and bedside reading matter while Harry burrowed under the bedclothes like a mischievous child trying to avoid a rampaging mother.

Mitchell's deputy, Malcolm Chalmers, authorised the use of axes on Sally's door. He obviously didn't hear her plaintive cry of 'Come in'. It could have been that the police enjoyed breaking the door down with an axe. In some way it gave a purpose to their day. As the dozen policemen poured into Sally's 12-foot-square garret their attention was taken, not by the two full-length mirrors or the impressive array of whips, canes and other instruments of torture displayed on a wallstand like snooker cues (one of Sally's regulars was a masochist who was a joiner – the fashioning of the stand was a genuine labour of love), but by the extraordinary sight of Sally sitting up in bed apparently deeply engrossed in 'The Denning Report'. This HMSO Government report on the Profumo Affair had been a best-seller at seven shillings and sixpence for months.

'Hello, Sally,' said Chalmers nonchalantly. 'Didn't know you wore glasses.'

'Hello, Sergeant. You back on the Vice again, then?'

'Detective Sergeant now,' said Chalmers, conscious that Sally was capable of saying something about their previous encounters that could embarrass him somewhat in front of his troops. 'Robbery Squad,' he added pointedly.

'You don't expect to find no-one here surely?'

Chalmers breathed a small inward sigh of relief. She obviously wasn't going to refer to their sordid past. He began again with the cat-and-mouse game he enjoyed so much. 'So, how long you been wearing them glasses?'

'I always worn 'em. Just took 'em off for the customers. Causes embarrassment otherwise.'

'We heard as how you was seeing this Great Train Robber,' said Chalmers hastily, anxious to steer the conversation into charted waters.

Sally laughed shortly. 'What? Buster Edwards? Here? You must be joking. Everyone knows about him and June.'

It was true. Buster's attachment to his wife was legendary throughout the underworld. Chalmers decided it was time to foreclose. Logically, Harry wouldn't be in the wardrobe. Even someone as inherently stupid as Harry Stenford wouldn't have done that. Chalmers strode forward and ripped the bedclothes off the bed. Sally shrieked instinctively and tried to cover her naked breasts with her hands. Also naked and crouched at the foot of the bed was Harry.

Chalmers looked at him impassively. 'Hello, Harry,' he said without a hint of surprise. 'You hid any of that two and half million quid up there?'

Less than thirty minutes later a handcuffed, surly Harry was standing in front of a triumphant Jack Mitchell. With the capture of Harry Stenford, Mitchell felt he was now breathing down the necks of Buster and Bruce. He gestured to Chalmers to leave them alone. Chalmers left with bad grace. He had made the arrest. He didn't see why he should be deprived of the fun of extracting the information from Harry. No doubt Mitchell would call him later if he needed to get down to the nitty-gritty.

Mitchell gazed soulfully at Harry for nearly a minute. Harry returned the stare unblinking. Mitchell got up and walked round the front of his desk. He decided to try the soft approach first.

'Hello, Harry.'

'Hello, Mr Mitchell.' Harry felt he was on safe ground here.

'You heard what's happened to your friends? We've got the lot. Pretty much. Upset some very important people, you have. You're going down for a hell of a stretch, son.'

Harry wondered where all this was leading. He knew, partly by instinct and partly because Bruce had always told him, that in a police interview the only possible route for him to take was almost total silence. If the police were going to fit him up they'd do it anyway. He'd never be able to convince them of his innocence by his articulate use of the English language. The logical recourse was to silence. Harry shrugged his shoulders.

Mitchell, in his turn, was wondering whether he should just tell Chalmers to work Harry over and extract an address. It was most unlikely that Harry could be out-manoeuvred in a battle of wits. He simply wouldn't understand what was going on so he wouldn't be able to play the game. Mitchell decided to be straight with the big man. 'You interested in releasing information about Bruce and Buster?'

Harry smiled. So that's what Mitchell wanted. Well, wild horses wouldn't make him tell where his two mates were holed up. The fact that he didn't know and therefore couldn't release the information was immaterial. Harry was going to enjoy obstructing the police in the course of their enquiries for as long as possible.

'You offering me a deal, Mr Mitchell?' asked Harry.

'Come on, Harry,' cajoled Mitchell. 'Be sensible. They'd shop you if they were here. They know the game.'

Harry was outraged at Mitchell's glibness. If he

had been at all unsure of the correct policy to adopt, that gratuitous insult confirmed that he had been right at the beginning.

Mitchell started to get rather edgy. 'Come on, Harry. Where are they? I want them.'

Harry continued to stare stoically ahead.

'Do I have to ask Wild Bill Chalmers to help persuade you?'

Harry glanced sideways at Mitchell, his eyes dancing with contempt for Mitchell's pathetic, half-veiled threat. 'Sorry, Mr Mitchell,' he reaffirmed, 'I don't know nothing.'

In Wraysbury June was using bedtime to instil into Nicky a sense of the changes that had befallen the family.

'And my name is . . .?' she asked for the fourth time in as many minutes.

'Katie,' replied Nicky promptly, her attention focussed on the faces Buster was making behind June's back.

'No. *Your* name is Katie. My name is . . .?'

'Pauline'.

'Pauline. Good girl.' June sighed. This was hard work and might even be critical at some stage. 'You Katie, me Pauline,' June reiterated. It served only as a cue for Buster to leap on her from behind and send all of them sprawling onto the bed with Buster yelling, 'Me Tarzan, you June.' After the tickling and the giggling had passed June sat up and looked hard at Buster, trying to ensure he would take this name-changing business seriously so as to impress the importance of it on Nicky.

'You not Tarzan. You not even Buster. You Jack – me Pauline,' but it merely prompted another outbreak of tickling from Buster's wandering fingers.

Later that night Buster was back on the indoor rowing machine, wearing his Stephanie Bowman plastic pants – a special pair of slimming shorts. June was trying to make sure that their efforts to evade capture went further than changing their names and Buster growing a moustache. She set him the target of losing thirty pounds in weight which would help to alter his appearance dramatically.

June came into the bedroom to find her husband sweating dutifully away. He eyed his late-night snack with alarm. 'More carrots and lettuce! I can't eat that stuff all the time. It's not fit for a growing boy.'

'Open wide,' said June and popped the first few carrot sticks into Buster's dry mouth. Buster thought longingly of the last fry-up he had eaten when meeting Bruce.

'You don't know what I'd give for a pint of beer and a plate of sausage and chips.'

'Yes, I do,' came the quick response. 'About three pounds round the middle. At least.'

Buster recognized a brick wall when he saw one. 'Thank you, Pauline Ryan.'

'It's a pleasure, Jack Ryan.'

It couldn't be denied, however, that June's methods were working. Buster lost over a stone in weight during the first three months at Wraysbury and though he wouldn't admit as much to June, he actually felt better for it. He still missed his cholesterol fix but he was learning to live without it and though life was mostly repetitive it had its moments of drama.

One morning he was toying with a huge 1000-piece jigsaw puzzle, a mental exercise he was learning to enjoy, when the doorbell rang. June ran into the room and drew back the thick lace curtain sufficiently to ascertain the identity of the person outside.

'It's Mrs Squires.'

'Who?'

'The landlady'.

'Jesus,' exclaimed Buster with irritation. He was just on the verge of getting all the edge pieces sorted out. He scuttled upstairs and into the bedroom as June walked slowly to the front door.

Mrs Squires was a rich, middle-aged woman who owned a number of properties in West London and beyond. It enabled her to keep an active interest in other people's affairs and provided her with a useful source of gossip. Although June was not to know this, she made a habit of calling on her tenants unexpectedly just to see what she could glean in the way of new information.

The justification of this current visit was to warn June that she had received a number of complaints from the neighbours about the state of the garden. June was aware of the horticultural disaster outside but neither she nor Buster were greatly motivated to do anything about it. They had never previously lived in a house with a garden attached to it. Such extravagances were few and far between in the impoverished area of South London in which they had both been raised.

June apologized as profusely as she could, standing there with the front door held open, hoping desperately that Mrs Squires would take the hint and make her visit a cursory one. Mrs Squires, however, had no such intention as her eyes drank in the changes made to her house.

'You don't mind if I look around do you? I do so love this house.'

She deliberately lowered her mongrel dog to the floor. It immediately headed for the staircase and Mrs Squires headed after it. With a sigh June closed the front door and hoped that Buster had heard enough of the conversation to take appropriate cover.

In fact Buster was fast asleep. Tired from his morning exertions with the rowing machine and the jigsaw puzzle he had retreated into the built-in wardrobe in the master bedroom with *Playboy* magazine and a torch. When Mrs Squires finally left, after a cup of very strong instant coffee, June raced upstairs to find the one true love of her life slumped inside the wardrobe, his mouth open, his torch illuminating the centrefold, snoring gently.

The conversation over lunch was a shade desultory. 'Well, I don't know how to do it, do I? I ain't never had no garden before.'

Buster was unimpressed. 'Well, I ain't never had no beard before, but you don't see me bellyaching.'

'I'll do you a deal, Buster,' offered June. 'You weed the garden and I'll weed your beard. Just as overgrown it is.' She giggled.

'Just get out there, you slagheap, and do something,' said Buster gallantly.

'I don't know what to do. I could be digging up some dehydrangea what's fifty years old.' June ascribed properties to plants that she knew belonged to trees – and antiques.

'If it's fifty years old it'll need digging up, won't it?'

Buster was worried about his image. 'I can't do it, can I? I mean, "Britain's most wanted criminal was arrested today while weeding the back garden"! Do me a favour!'

June threw up her hands in despair. 'Well, what *are* we going to do? We can't have a gardener in and if we don't do something we'll have the neighbours round. Shall I ring Jimmy?'

'Jesus! Jimmy's job is to get us passports, get us

out of the country, protect us from the Law. He's not there to mow the bleeding grass.'

June looked depressed.

Buster had an idea. 'Ain't there a gardening book in the house? Old biddy like that – she's bound to have one.'

Buster was right. One of the very few books on Mrs Squire's small bookcase was a book of flowers and shrubs. The two of them looked through it and decided on their course of action. June with a scarf over her head went into the garden and tapped each plant in turn with the trowel. Buster would then look at it through a pair of powerful binoculars and riffle through the pages of the gardening book. If he could find it in the book he would shake his head and she would pass on to the next flower or shrub. Whenever he could find no reference to it in Mrs Squire's book he would give the thumbs up sign to June who would dig up the offending weed and drop it into a cardboard box. The two of them enjoyed themselves hugely, laughing constantly at the ludicrousness of their plight. In particular it occurred to them both simultaneously that this act of idiocy was in some measure the result of June's long-expressed desire for a nice house in the country. If only Jack Mitchell and the Robbery Squad who were pursuing them with such fanatical vengeance could see them now!

CHAPTER ELEVEN

Sir James McDowell emerged from the crowded Old Vic foyer to find that during the seemingly interminable time he had spent in the theatre it had started to rain. He was even more aggrieved to discover that the limousine, that should have been waiting for him right outside the front door as arranged, was in fact parked some way down the Waterloo Road. Sir James hadn't enjoyed watching Peter O'Toole as Hamlet. He had liked the actor in *Lawrence of Arabia,* but a schoolboy aversion to Shakespeare and a civil servant's disdain for the Arts combined to make four hours of tedium for him.

He thus approached his meeting at the Reform Club with Mr Justice Parry in a filthy temper. The two had agreed to meet for a nightcap at their club, which they did with some frequency. McDowell was thawing out by the blaze of a roaring fire, having already downed one agreeable brandy, when Parry approached to find his companion immersed in the early editions of the morning papers.

'Pleased to see there's no Richie Benaud this time.'

Parry admitted to being puzzled by the statement.

'Australian cricketer. Shrewd captain. They've just announced the names of the party to tour England this summer.'

'Ahh.' Parry brightened at the prosaic explanation. He thought for a moment he had been missing something. 'Never cared much for cricket myself. I was a wet bob.'

The two were now talking the specialist language of the British public schools.

'Eton?' enquired McDowell.

'Radley,' replied Parry.

'Ah. Thought I didn't remember you there.'

'My youngest son starts there in September,' said Parry, content to keep the conversation rolling along agreed lines. It was up to McDowell to lead it.

'You must have enjoyed your time there, then,' McDowell commented, revealing no urgency in getting to the nub of the matter.

'God, no! Hated it. Didn't you? Still, taught me a thing or two, I can tell you.'

'Perhaps we might start sentencing some of our criminal fraternity to seven years in a good Public School. That would sort them out fast enough.'

Parry chuckled at the prospect. 'Doubt they could take it. Remember the cold showers?'

McDowell shuddered. He remembered all right. 'And the beatings. Nightmare.'

Parry felt impelled to say something about the efficacy of the birch for the criminal classes as proved by its retention in the very best schools but he refrained because of his knowledge of Sir James's bachelor existence. You couldn't always tell with such people how many of the noble traditions of the Public Schools still held people like that in thrall. Besides he thought he caught the drift. 'You think we should start with the Train Robbers, then?'

McDowell didn't answer for a moment. He let his eye wander down the leader page of the *Daily Telegraph*, glad of the fact that Parry had been so quick on the uptake. 'General feeling in the Government is fairly hostile.' McDowell lowered his paper and almost for the first time looked directly at the judge. 'Can you have a word in the right ear? Don't like to interfere at Crown Court level myself.'

'Oh, I quite understand.' Parry preened himself

with his dexterity of mind. 'Any particular figure in mind?'

Again McDowell paused. When the figure had been suggested to him he had reacted with the surprise of a human being rather than that of a senior Whitehall Mandarin.

'The thought was suggested – thirty.'

Parry was genuinely astonished. His mouth didn't exactly fall open but the tension in his jaw certainly slackened, observed McDowell, with satisfaction.

'Thirty!' echoed Parry. 'Somebody must be very cross.'

McDowell thought he had better emphasize where his own feelings in this matter lay. 'Well, there's likely to be an election in the autumn. Must re-establish some sort of authority after all that hoo-hah last year. Wouldn't have given a fig for our chances when Alec took over. I must say I rather thought it was going be RAB this time but you must admit Alec's done awfully well.'

'Oh, agreed. Absolutely,' blustered Parry while he tried to think of the legal implications of such a sentence, never mind the public outcry. 'Thirty years for robbery. Bit steep, don't you think?'

McDowell regarded Parry with a steely countenance. The man was soft. 'Not really, no. So your son starts in September, eh? What is he? Classicist?'

'Of course.' The conversation was back on the rails again. Parry projected a natural sequence of events. 'Bit of luck, he could be reading Greats at Christ Church.'

Some months after this conversation nine men stood in the dock in the county town of Aylesbury, the capital, as it were, of the county in which the Great Train Robbery had taken place. The Assize Court itself was too small for such a major trial so it was held in the recently-built chamber of the Rural District Council which had been converted into a court especially for the occasion. The robbers were hoping that the trial would be held in London. They felt they would be better understood by a jury of Londoners. Perhaps precisely for this reason the trial took place in Aylesbury where the jury was less likely to be subject to undue pressures.

The authorities made it quite clear how much time and effort had been expanded in bringing these monstrous men to account. There had been 120 officers working on the case; 1700 exhibits had been prepared for presentation in court; and over 2300 written statements had been taken from relevant witnesses. Mr Justice Edmund Davies took six working days to deliver his summary. Eventually, after the jury had retired for just over forty-eight hours, they reappeared with the verdict that everyone had felt had been inevitable since before the trial had even opened. With the odd technical exception, all the robbers on trial were found guilty of conspiracy to rob and of armed robbery.

The length of sentences had long been the subject of speculation. The average had been about fifteen years but Bruce felt that they might be longer. He understood well enough that without Buster and himself, everyone was aware that the job was not yet over. An example had to be made of the men in custody so that the official thirst for revenge was slaked and so that the rest of the criminal fraternity would think again before offering further aid to Buster and Bruce.

The convicted men were transferred from the modern atmosphere of the Council Chamber back to the old Assize Court for sentencing. In this depressing and forbidding building, the presiding judge seated on his throne beneath a large royal coat of arms delivered an appropriately mediaeval sentence. For conspiracy to rob the sentence was twenty-five years. For the crime of armed robbery itself the sentence was thirty years. Though they were to run concurrently it still meant that they would be in prison for a minimum of over twenty years. When they emerged their children would be grown up and their wives or girlfriends would be old women. Their lives were effectively over.

Buster and June heard the news at first on the radio but for some reason they didn't trust their ears. It only really sank in when the paper-boy arrived with that night's copy of the *Evening Standard*. They read the headline '307 YEARS!' over and over again without talking. Finally Buster hurled down the paper in rage and frustration.

'Thirty years for robbery! It's a bleeding disgrace!'

'You realize they'd have got off lighter if they bleeding killed someone? More than a life sentence, that is,' concurred Jimmy.

June worried more about their own predicament. 'We'll never do a deal with the Law now.'

She had always hoped against hope that the police would revert to their traditional ways, when a large sum of money in untraceable used notes, wrapped up inside a brown paper bag, could produce quite miraculous results. Buster had been telling her that such a hope was unrealistic on this occasion, but it was only that copy of the *Evening Standard* that actually brought it home to them all.

'I ain't never known a time when Old Bill wouldn't do no deals,' complained Buster. 'It's all that Profumo mess. That's what done it. Bleeding world's turned upside down now.'

'Thirty years in prison,' echoed June, her pretty

face still pale at the prospect. 'They'll be over sixty before they come out.'

'They're hard men, June,' said Jimmy in an attempt to cheer them both up. 'They'll make it.'

But June wasn't to be comforted so easily. 'What about Harry?' she asked. 'He's already in solitary.'

Buster continued to pace round the room like a caged animal. His philosophising was primitive but pointed. 'You screw some tart who gives all the country's secrets to the Russians and you don't get invited to no big parties no more. Nick a few quid from a train and you do thirty years in stir. It's wicked, it is.'

June and Jimmy didn't contradict him. Buster had articulated both their thoughts. All right maybe they had nicked more than just a few quid but that was the game. The game of cops and robbers had always been played according to a naturally-evolving set of rules. The sentences passed at Aylesbury, no doubt initiated by a frightened Tory Government, had broken those rules. It was the unfairness of it all that hurt so much.

The sentences that had infuriated Buster and Bruce and terrified their women failed to save Richard Poyser from the sack. He had been unable to produce the two ringleaders and he was the obvious candidate for scapegoat. He was cleaning out the drawers of his desk when Jack Mitchell tapped lightly and entered. He made Mitchell wait for a full thirty seconds before looking up and acknowledging his presence. It was to be his last triumph.

He looked carefully at his junior officer, pushed his chair back and moved over to the window with its seductive view down the Victoria Embankment. Eventually, he spoke quietly, still with his back to Mitchell. 'Seems like thirty years wasn't enough.'

Mitchell, who had no idea why he had been summoned to Poyser's office, simply requested elucidation.

'Those thirty-year sentences,' explained Poyser. 'Not enough to save me. They're calling it "early retirement". Well, sounds better than the boot doesn't it, Jack?'

Mitchell, though not one of Poyser's greatest admirers, was nevertheless suprised at this new turn of events. 'But we got them all, sir. All of them. Except Reynolds and Edwards.'

Poyser smiled sadly. 'It was Reynolds and Edwards that did for me in the end. Who would have thought that a couple of small-time villains like them . . .' He broke off as the injustice of it all swept over him again. He sublimated it into a slow-burning anger directed against Mitchell. 'I gather you've been speaking directly to the Commissioner. Without consulting me.'

Mitchell flushed. It was true that he had spoken to Poyser's boss, but he could hardly refuse to answer the Commissioner's direct questions about Edwards and Reynolds, and though he knew he had no alternative, he also knew this particular repercussion was in some manner inevitable.

'He asked me about Reynolds and Edwards, sir.' Like Harry Stenford, Mitchell reckoned the less said the better. It was a 'no win' situation for him.

'Well, you obviously told him what he wanted to hear,' snapped Poyser. 'He wants you in sole charge of arresting the two of them. Well done.'

There was a distinct lack of warmth in the Assistant Commissioner's voice. Mitchell felt that any attempt to accept or reject the 'compliment' would be misinterpreted. He chose to remain silent.

After a moment Poyser returned to the contents of

his drawers. 'You'll find me at Lords if you should ever want the benefit of my thirty years on the Force.' He looked up. He couldn't help but feel the irony. 'Funny, that. Thirty years I've been here. Ring a bell?' Mitchell felt the question was rhetorical. He allowed Poyser to continue.

Poyser was a decent man. He loved his cricket and his mind wandered back to the halcyon days of Middlesex cricket just after the war when he spent all his spare time at Lords. He found the comparison with the utilitarian side of 1963 to be depressing. He smiled ruefully at Mitchell.

'Wouldn't mind if they had a decent side. Not like the '47 team. Robertson, Compton, Edrich, Robbins, that lot . . .'

Mitchell looked at him blankly. Poyser could have been talking Chinese, for all he understood. Poyser broke off, shrugged his shoulders and slipped into retirement.

The two men who had been responsible for Poyser's early retirement, and who were to become the fixation of Jack Mitchell's life, were pacing the deserted wharf of the docks in Rotherhithe. Buster was becoming obsessed again with the possibility of doing a deal with the police. Somehow if £10,000 in untraceable banknotes could find their way into the right pocket he was still convinced that the Law would turn a blind eye, maybe co-operate in a reduced sentence. Bruce tried hard to make Buster believe that this one was different. Certain police officers, who were well-known for being approachable in this manner, could no longer protect the robbers. The crime was too big, too successful and too hard for the Establishment to take. If nine men were serving sentences of up to thirty years, Buster was living in a fool's paradise if he really believed he could get away with eighteen months and an endorsement on his driving licence.

'You think Mitchell'd be interested? Now he's the gaffer?'

Bruce sighed. Why didn't he ever *listen*? 'Ain't gonna be no deals, Buster. I told you before.'

'Just that June's not all that keen on Mexico.'

So that was it. After all that bullshit, Buster was still worried about his wife.

'June again! Shit, Buster. Who's wearing the trousers in your house?'

This time Buster was waiting for him. 'Lot of the time, Bruce, ain't neither of us. We're getting on really well these days. No distractions.'

Buster had won that exchange fairly comfortably. There was a pause while Bruce regrouped for the next attack. 'Does she know what the Law's like at the moment? If we'd taken the Crown Jewels they couldn't be coming after us harder.'

'I know that. But June's mother . . .' Buster broke off when he recalled Bruce's previously expressed opinion of June's mother.

Bruce couldn't suppress a smile. Getting Buster to bring June or her mother into the argument was in itself a triumph for him. 'Look, I got it all set up. Franny's going ahead to make sure Old Bill won't follow. She'll be in Acapulco in a couple of weeks.'

'Where's that, then?' Buster was genuinely unsure.

'Mexico, you ignorant sod.'

There was a pause while Buster thought ironically about his dream of success – the sun, the sea, the women, the good life. While he was living in South London with no real prospect of making it come true, the vision was enticing, almost obsessive. Now that he desperately needed to be in that sunshine paradise, just to preserve his own freedom, he was assailed by doubts of a staggeringly mundane nature.

'When you off then?' asked Bruce, puncturing the gloomy silence that had settled over them as they continued to pace the deserted wharf.

'Don't know exactly. June hates abroad.' Buster tried one last despairing throw of the dice. 'You reckon even if we gave them the lot there'd be no deal?'

Bruce exploded. When would the guy listen? 'No deals this time, Buster. Don't waste your breath thinking about it. We can't hardly get outside the front door these days. Look how long it took to arrange meetings like this.'

Bruce calmed down. He was fond of his old mate and it was apparent that it was up to him to persuade him to get out of the country as fast as possible. 'You want to go down for the full thirty like the others?'

Buster's gloom deepened. He'd already heard stories of how their mates had been sent to different prisons, tossed into solitary confinement, put into maximum security wings, treated worse than spies who had been caught working for Russia, like Blake and Lonsdale. The enjoyment of the notoriety soon wore off. What remained was the feeling communicated to them by the behaviour of the authorities that the Train Robbers were pariahs, beyond the pale even in prison. He wondered how anyone could face that prospect for thirty years.

'Just think about Mexico,' coaxed Bruce. 'The sun, the sand, the booze, the birds.' Bruce's mind wandered sensuously over the prospect of the sexual cornucopia he saw in the distance.

'All that crumpet, Buster. Just waiting for you to show up and grab handfuls of it.' His hands shaped the outline of two breasts. He looked at Buster and grinned conspiratorially, but it was dark and anyway Buster was thinking about June. This wouldn't really be the right sort of argument to use to clinch matters with her. 'It's that dream, Buster. That dream what we worked all our lives for.'

Buster turned his face to Bruce and shook his head philosophically. 'Yeh. It's what I told June. Don't make no difference, though. Women's funny like that. Know what I mean?'

That was the last time Bruce and Buster managed to meet before Bruce slipped quietly out of the country in a specially-rented small craft. He landed on the shores of France just outside Dunkirk and was sped away by a friend in a waiting sports car down Route Nationale 7 to a villa between Antibes and Juan-les-Pins. He remained there for six weeks until arrangements were made for a smooth passage to Acapulco.

Back in Britain Buster fretted about the best course of action for June and himself. Any doubts he might have entertained about the advisability of remaining in the country were swept away when he heard that Fairclough had been ostentatiously arrested in the grounds of one of the Inns of Court.

Jack Mitchell was determined not to go the way of Poyser. The public arrest of a practising barrister not only turned up the heat under Buster and Bruce but it demonstrated to the general public, his own bosses and to the politicians that effective action was being taken.

A furious Fairclough was paraded in his office. Mitchell gestured for the accompanying officer to release the handcuffs and to leave the prisoner with Chalmers and himself.

'Well, Mr Fairclough, sir. Very surprised to find you in this situation,' he said as the door closed.

'Inspector, this whole thing has been the most ghastly mistake. I did try telling the sergeant here . . .'

'Not my job, sir, listening,' cut in Chalmers cryptically.

'In any case, this so-called crime I'm being accused of committing . . .'

This time it was Mitchell who interrupted the flow. 'Conspiring to construct a knowingly false alibi for a criminal is a serious offence, sir.'

'Very angry man is Mr Shipton,' added Chalmers.

'Shipton!' exploded Fairclough in disbelief. He couldn't believe the police were stitching him up like this. 'You're prepared to take that crook's word against that of a graduate of Trinity College, Oxford?'

Under pressure Fairclough's upper-class credentials were invariably presented for inspection. Mitchell raised his eyebrows as if he didn't understand the non-sequitur. 'I'm a Hendon man myself,' he confessed. Memories of student days in the Police College in North-West London flooded back. He decided they couldn't compete satisfactorily with Fairclough's days in the City of Dreaming Spires and didn't pursue the analogy.

Now that he had got Fairclough on the run Mitchell pressed home the advantage. 'That's for a jury to decide – whose word to take. We just have our job to do.'

'But you're on the Robbery Squad. This has got nothing to do . . .' He broke off abruptly as the light finally dawned. Shipton had been a former client and there had been a number of unpleasant incidents during his defence which culminated in their losing the case and Shipton serving three years in Strangeways. Fairclough finally realized that his current predicament had indeed got nothing whatsoever to do with the charge they were trying to level at him.

'Oh. I see,' he said rather miserably.

Mitchell smiled. He shared the general feeling of the world about Fairclough. He couldn't deny that he was positively revelling in the man's discomfort. At least Buster and Bruce were honest-to-goodness criminals. They didn't try to play both sides of the street like this one.

'I don't want to be greedy,' he said evenly. 'Edwards *or* Reynolds. I don't care which.'

Fairclough was silent. This was a big decision. Not which one of course. Both Buster and Bruce had sufficient friends of an aggressive nature that they would have no hesitation in wreaking revenge in the most primitive and violent way. He had to decide whether it was more desirable to hand over one of the robbers and depart on a long, possibly permanent, holiday abroad or take his chances in prison. The police weren't bluffing.

'What's the going rate for perverting the course of Justice. Chalmers?' Mitchell thought he would speed up the decision-making process.

'Five or six years. If he goes to Parkhurst we could arrange a little spell in the maximum security wing with one of them Train Robbers.'

Mitchell looked as though the thought had never crossed his mind before. 'That's right. Oh, they'll be very pleased to see you again.'

It worked. Fairclough made his choice.

'I don't know where Edwards or Reynolds is. You must believe me, Inspector.' Fairclough's voice rose half an octave as his advocacy took on new heights of passion and commitment. 'There's a fellow that works for them. As a sort of legitimate front. Jimmy the Nose he's called . . .'

CHAPTER TWELVE

Later that same night Jimmy the Nose was tying up the boat at the jetty that ran from the bottom of the garden at Buster's rented house in Wraysbury out into the River Thames. After much prevaricating, it had been decided that Buster would go by himself to Switzerland, sort out the money and the passports, have an operation to change the shape of his nose and then send for June.

June had only agreed with extreme reluctance to this scheme. She hated the prospect of separation from Buster at the best of times – and this was not the best of times. She begged to be allowed to go along with him but had eventually accepted the argument that she should wait in seclusion in England until the time was right for her and Nicky to join Buster. Now that the time had arrived for the two to part she was no longer convinced that this was the right course of action.

She clung to Buster's arm as she fought unsuccessfully to restrain the tears that were welling up in her eyes. Buster did his best to comfort her.

'Come on, June, just think about Mexico. The dream eh? The sun, the sea, the good life!'

June couldn't. 'I don't want you to go, Buster. I'd rather take the risk.'

'You can't mean that, June. Me and Bruce, we're the only ones left on the trot. Mitchell'd give his granny to get us – he'd give anyone's granny.'

June shook her head stubbornly, reiterating the old argument. 'I want us to go together. We belong together.'

Buster refrained from the impatient outburst that was on the tip of his tongue. Now that the decision had been taken he just wanted to get going. It was typical of women that June should choose this moment to change her mind.

'It's too dodgy. You're safe here,' he began. 'Jimmy'll look after you – just like he's always done. And your mum'll be here to keep you company. You're safe and it's easier for me to travel alone. Safer all round. Trust me.' He kissed her tenderly and held her face between his hands. 'Next time you see me I'll have my conk all altered. Bleeding Mr Kennington 1965 – that's me.'

June remained unconvinced. 'What if something happens? What if I ain't never gonna see you no more?'

It was not a question to which Buster could easily offer an answer. Fortunately Jimmy had walked up to meet them from the jetty and greeted them both affectionately.

'All ready, Buster. We'd better get going. Boat leaves St Katharine's dock for Antwerp at midnight.'

'How long, Buster? How long will it all take?'

'Dunno yet. Maybe six weeks for the passports and to get the money going nice and easy from here to Zurich to the Bahamas and on to Acapulco. I'm seeing the nose doctor on Friday. Maybe he can do the operation next day. I'll get word to you.'

June did not look comforted.

'Don't worry, June. It's all going to be OK. Everything's under control.'

June nodded glumly. Buster started to kiss her. June responded with passion. Jimmy felt a trifle embarrassed although he knew of his friends' deep love for each other. In addition he was worried about the connection at the dock in the Port of London. The cargo boat on which he had secured passage out of the country for Buster wouldn't wait beyond the pre-arranged midnight deadline for sailing.

'Buster, come on,' he urged. 'It's getting late. He'll leave without you if you're not there.'

The lovers separated.

'Buster, don't go!' The note of hysteria was creeping into June's voice. 'I'm so frightened. I love you so much.'

Buster tried one last tactic to disengage himself as neatly as possible without damaging his wife's feelings. 'Now listen to me, you old bag. I been shut up with you twenty-four hours a bleeding day, seven days a bleeding week for months now. Most men would've throttled their wives by now. Only reason I ain't – I think you're the best sodding thing that ever happened to me.'

Buster kissed her for the last time and broke away. He and Jimmy walked down the garden path and clambered into the launch that was to take them eastwards down the Thames. As Jimmy untied the mooring rope and cast off Buster called softly back to June, 'Kiss Nicky goodbye for me.' It was said with such infinite tenderness that June broke out in goosebumps. She nodded, trying to blink back the inevitable tears.

The launch chugged its way out into the mainstream of the river and headed off eastwards. Buster stood looking at his wife silhouetted against the stark outline of the house. Even though her features had become indistinguishable in the darkness he felt strongly that she was the most beautiful woman in the world. They had been married for fifteen years but June's appeal for him had rarely diminished. He knew he was lucky in this respect. He watched his other friends who found the uncritical admiration of young women an irresistible turn-on. He experienced the occasional pang of envy as he saw them leave the nightclub shepherding the latest blond, long-legged captive in arrogantly proprietorial manner but he had always known the real worth of June's deep and abiding love for him. Not that he had been a saint himself, of course. But his falls from grace were few and far between, to be followed by such feelings of guilt and self-loathing that it took him months to understand why he had even bothered with anyone else for five minutes.

June watched the receding figure of her husband until the boat rounded a bend and was lost to view. She had always known of his occasional indiscretion, and though nothing was ever said between them they were so close that words were unnecessary. Buster's emotions were all on the surface. It was his warmth, his humour, his generosity that had made such an impact on her when they had first met soon after the end of the war. His drift into crime rather than look for some form of legitimate, badly-paid work had never greatly disturbed her. His lavish demonstrations of affection on the rare occasions when he had struck it lucky she found charming if a little birdbrained. In short she loved Buster as much as she ever had. With all his many imperfections she preferred him to any other man she had ever met.

June shivered as a blast of night air sent a sudden damp chill through her body. She gathered her shawl about her and retreated to the inviting, lighted French windows of the lounge. She couldn't help smiling at the irony. This beautiful, remote, detached house in Wraysbury was the ideal house she had dreamed of when stuck behind the settee with Buster and Nicky trying to avoid the rent man and his collection days. Now that they had acquired the house they couldn't live there even though they now had the means for the first time in their lives to buy it. Instead, circumstances had conspired to send them all on an adventure round the world when she would far rather have been safely back in England, preferably close to her mother and the Elephant and Castle district of London. Still she knew her place. It was, as ever, beside her husband.

Early the next morning the Belgian freighter steamed slowly into the port of Antwerp. In the grey light of dawn Buster, dressed in the nondescript navy-blue roll-top sweater of a merchant seaman trooped down the gangplank with a dozen sailors. He peeled away from the group and walked swiftly towards a Mercedes which was waiting for him in the designated area of the wharf. He opened the rear door and slid in. Inside the sleek German car was a blond attractive German woman named Irma. Buster smiled warmly at her, pleased that the arrangements made by Jimmy in England and communicated to him in the depths of Wraysbury had worked so well.

There was no answering smile. Irma drew a familiar-looking dark blue stiffbacked British passport from her handbag and gave it to Buster. Buster was appalled at the crude forgery. It was nothing more than a passport in the name of 'Miller' with Buster's own photograph pasted on top.

'Christ! This is awful!'

Irma shrugged. 'I am called Irma.'

Buster was still turning the passport over and over. 'Yeh, I know. They told me in London. Look, this is crap. I can't get away with this.'

Irma didn't seem to share Buster's concern. 'Is OK for this border.'

'You'd better be right, Charlie.'

Fortunately for Buster the cool German woman

seemed to know her borders all right. Neither set of customs officials seemed remotely interested in them as the large Mercedes was waved through the barriers quite casually. Buster heaved a large inward sigh of relief. He turned to face the woman again.

'What about the Swiss bank account and the operation?'

Irma looked away, in some discomfort, as if she were disguising the real origin of the problems. 'I need more money.'

Buster exploded. 'More! Jesus Christ! I paid already. I paid those bastards in London!'

Irma refused to meet his eyes. Dully she repeated the request for more money. 'Three thousand pounds.'

'Three grand?' echoed Buster in astonishment. 'Piss off, Kraut.' Buster's natural xenophobia reasserted itself. He thought back to the war. He wondered what Irma was doing when the Nazis were in power. He then realized that she would have been an infant in arms during that time. His thoughts switched to Irma's father who must surely have been a leading member of the Waffen SS when he slowly became aware that the car had ceased travelling. The driver, in conscientious German fashion, had pulled the car over to the side of the autobahn, switched off the engine and turned to face his passengers. He was now holding a gun which he was pointing directly at Buster. He released the safety catch and closed one eye. The barrel was two feet away from its target. Buster shrugged resignedly. He was getting used to being ripped off, even if it wasn't usually as blatant as this one. He started to open the duffel bag he was carrying.

Two days later he was sitting in the smartly-furnished waiting-room of a private clinic outside Dusseldorf reading with no little bewilderment the West German equivalent of *Woman's Own*. Irma had been gone a worrying fifteen minutes. When she returned, wearing what Buster now recognized as a permanent look of anxiety, she beckoned him to rise and follow her which Buster did. When they were in the corridor Irma relayed the bad news.

'Is no good here.'

'You what?'

'Doctor says you have no need of operation.'

'What a cheek! It's *my* conk. Why can't I do what I want with it?'

Further protestation proved pointless. Together they left the smart modern clinic of the wealthy German cosmetic surgeon with a conscience, and drove across town into the area of Dusseldorf which Buster instantly recognized was the equivalent of impoverished Kennington or Vauxhall. Eventually they drew up outside a private house which contained one room which had been converted into the nose-job equivalent of a back-street abortion clinic.

Buster listened with alarm as Irma and the doctor, a large unkempt man with a dirty white coat and a face that might have belonged to a professional boxer, spoke rapidly to each other in German while looking all the time at Buster. The subject of their conversation was meanwhile looking round the room and noticing a large number of photographs of women with large breasts. 'If the man makes noses for a living why don't he start on himself?' wondered Buster before his fertile imagination turned the man into the sort of doctor who operated on concentration-camp victims for the pure fun of the exercise.

The doctor grinned evilly at Buster and tapped him pointedly, not to say painfully, on the nose. 'So, *diese*

Nase nicht wahr?' he grinned at Irma who nodded silently in response. The doctor looked thoughtfully at Buster for a moment before gabbling away in German.

Buster felt distinctly uncomfortable. ''Ere, what's he on about, then?' he asked with alarm.

'Is OK,' volunteered Irma. 'Is good doctor.'

The doctor looked at Buster and then grinned evilly at the prospective patient before trying out his English, which presumably hadn't had an airing since the de-Nazification process he had cheated his way through in 1946.

'Unfortunately I am not doing many noses since many years. In 1945 vas sehr popular. I made the nose from Martin Borman. *Sie kennen* Martin Borman?'

Buster nodded. He had no idea what he was replying to but the doctor looked suitably pleased and launched into an impassioned defence of the remaining Nazi officials in hiding in South America. Buster continued to nod away and grin, ingratiating himself with the doctor though unable to understand a word of the German coming his way.

The doctor paused as his eye was caught by one of the framed photographs on his desk. He shook his head sadly. 'Now is all breasts. Like Marilyn Monroe.'

A spasm of cold fear shot through Buster. Just what did this doctor have in mind for him? He dimly remembered a passing phenomenon called April Ashley who a few months before had undergone a sex change operation though whether it was from man to woman or vice versa he couldn't remember. Was this what Irma and the Doctor had been discussing? He had heard horror stories before about the difficulties of translation and of course June had been fond of telling him stories from the newspapers which had revealed tragedies like the man who had the wrong leg amputated. If that could happen in England where patient and doctor spoke the same language what terrible fate awaited him in this country of the quick incision?

'But I don't want breasts like Marilyn Monroe,' he blustered quickly. 'Be a hell of a shock to June,' he added inanely.

The reply failed to halt the doctor in his tracks. He approached the terrified Englishman with a small stainless steel instrument with which he started to tap Buster's nose all the way from the bridge to the nostrils. From the next room it appeared as though the volume on the transistor radio had been turned up in anticipation of an imminent invasion. The music could have been Wagner or something stirringly martial – the sort that gets played on the radio during a coup d'état, or, thought Buster, the Blitzkrieg of Poland. He squirmed in his seat. 'Here, what you doing? Bleeding Nazi! You leave my conk alone.'

Ironically, with the two wanted train robbers safely out of the country the heat intensified under Jimmy and June. Jimmy soon got word that the police were looking to question him, and even though they had already pulled him in twice previously he didn't care to hang around to find out precisely what information the treacherous Fairclough had already passed on.

He bade farewell to June and went to live in a crofter's cottage in the North-West of Scotland, some twenty miles beyond Fort William, but Mitchell had managed to whip his Robbery Squad into shape and within a few weeks Jimmy was in the interview room at Scotland Yard helping the police with their enquiries. Mitchell, predictably, failed to extract much from him about Buster's movements. He tried a different tack, reminding him of the crushing sentences the convicted robbers had already received.

'You're a complete arsehole if you think that juries have changed in the last six months,' he began.

'I wasn't at that farm,' repeated Jimmy doggedly, 'And you can't fit me up and you know it.'

'We'll nail you on being an accessory after the fact, aiding and abetting a Great Train Robber. You'll go down for twenty, easy.'

Jimmy laughed but it was a hollow laugh. In normal circumstances Mitchell wouldn't even bother bringing the case to court. But these weren't normal circumstances and they both knew it.

'Fifty quid says it's less than five years.'

Mitchell smiled with satisfaction. 'I hate to take your money, friend, but I just might recognize where the banknotes came from.'

June continued to lead the modest existence in Wraysbury she had begun with Buster many months before. Her mother, who couldn't help enjoying the luxury of the large house and the company of the two people she cared most about in the world, did most of the shopping and collecting of Nicky from school. June found herself retreating into the sort of self-imposed isolation that had previously been Buster's fate.

One afternoon Mrs Barker complained of a cold and June set off to the local primary school to wait for Nicky's emergence shortly after 3.30. It was a grey, miserable day with heavy oppressive clouds, a cloying humidity and the prospect of imminent rain. Nicky came hurtling out of the school playground clutching a painting of a cow in a meadow with a sun the size of an atomic explosion.

'Hello, darling. Nice day?' asked June lifting her into her arms and kissing her.

Nicky thrust the painting at her and shook her head fiercely. 'Daniel Curtis was horrible to me.'

'Why?'

'Don't know.'

The conversation seemed to peter out at this point and the two set off for home until Nicky was suddenly shaken by sobs. June stopped and held her daughter close.

'What was it, darling? That horrible Daniel Curtis?'

The memory of whatever it was that Daniel had perpetrated was enough to induce a fresh outburst of hysteria.

'Don't cry, darling. All boys are horrible.'

'No they're not. I like Timothy Winters. He gave me a lick of his lolly.'

June applied the age-old remedy for a five-year-old's distress. 'Would you like some sweets, darling?'

Miraculously the tears stopped. It was as if a switch had been pulled. Nicky nodded coyly and buried her face in her mother's bosom.

They walked slowly towards the small sub-post office which was invariably submerged by school-children at this time of day. As they neared the shop the rain which had been threatening for some time suddenly started. A dozen large drops were followed by a cloudburst. The rain came down like stair rods, quickly filling the gutters and rushing towards the drains. June, holding Nicky, tumbled into the shop, the two of them shaking the rain off them as best they could.

'Ooh, it's gone all down my neck,' complained Nicky loudly, to the irritation of two middle-aged women who were painstakingly examining the limited supply of birthday cards, rather in the manner of serious browsers reading in an academic bookshop.

Nicky's attention was suddenly taken by the huge array of sweets on display in front of her. 'I want those and those and those and those' she demanded.

June laughed nervously. The atmosphere in the post office was getting to her. 'All your teeth'll fall out if you have that lot.'

'I don't mind.'

The old lady who was obviously the sub-post mistress finished tacking up yet another bureaucratic notice about social security benefits and turned to face her new customer. As she did so she revealed behind her a 'Wanted' poster of Buster and June. It was June before she had started to wear her black wig but it was easily recognizable, nevertheless. For a second June was frozen with horror. Dimly she heard Nicky's voice breaking into her consciousness. 'I want the chocolate buttons, Mum.'

Though it took only a fraction of a second, it appeared to June to take a superhuman effort to drag her own attention back to the mundane scene being played out in front of her. 'Do you want the chocolate buttons, darling?' she asked, as if Nicky had never suggested them, 'or would you like some jelly babies instead?'

With that sixth sense that all children possess at birth, the one that searches out and seizes on the slightest weakness in parental authority, Nicky zoomed remorselessly in on her mother's perceived wavering.

'Both,' she demanded brightly, all thoughts of the humiliations previously imposed on her by the unspeakable Daniel Curtis now long forgotten.

June smiled as warmly as she knew how at the old lady behind the counter. She wasn't smiling on the poster. Maybe it would help. June extracted her least Cockney voice and tried to confide in the old woman.

'Isn't it difficult when they go on like that?'

'I've got a grandchild just the same.'

'Oh, really?' June was full of enthusiastic interest. 'How old is she?'

The old lady was carefully measuring the sweets onto the aluminium scale. 'It's a boy, actually. Colin, lovely little thing. Well,' she admitted with a half smile, 'you always say that about your own, don't you? He's four.'

'Starting school, then, soon?' asked June, her eyes drawn to the hypnotically-slow operation in front of her.

'Oh, he's already at nursery school. He starts at Bernards Heath in September. Is that where your little girl is?'

'No,' said June shortly as she observed the final twirl of the paper bags. 'How much do I owe you?'

'Fourpence each,' said the old lady, turning round to check the price on the sweet jar labels and giving June acute anxiety as the poster swung into her line of vision again. 'So that's just eightpence, please.'

June scrabbled in her purse looking for a sixpence and two coppers that would avoid the need for change.

'I haven't seen you in here before, have I?' asked the woman, as June's paralysed fingers found the missing penny.

June slid the money across the counter, dropped the sweets in her handbag and grabbed Nicky whose eyes were rivetted by the picture of her father and mother.

'Mum? Isn't that . . .' she began but was cut off by June's firm declaration of 'Now you can have the sweets after your tea.'

Nicky was outraged by this betrayal and screamed her objections very loudly as she was dragged out of the shop and back into the rain, disapproving glances from the ranks of the birthday-card browsers following their retreating backs.

They raced home as fast as they could, Nicky enjoying being carried in such an exciting manner, June with her thoughts fixed on the piece of paper in the hall cupboard on which was written Jimmy's contact number in Scotland. She was in the middle of dialling when her mother emerged from the kitchen, looking pale.

'Take Nicky and give her some tea will you, Mum? I've got to get hold of Jimmy.'

'Ain't no use you trying to ring him, June.'

June looked up sharply, responding less to her mother's words than the sombre tone in which they had been delivered. 'What is it?' she asked, scared.

'On the wireless, half an hour ago. Suspected of helping one of the Great Train Robbers.'

The receiver dropped from June's lifeless hand.

Two days later they got word from Buster. The nose operation was completed and June could take a scheduled British European Airways flight to Zurich where Buster would meet her and Nicky. June was a bundle of nerves. Her mother made the booking for her.

For two hours before the taxi was due to arrive she wandered disconsolately in and out of the five bedrooms in the house, wondering whether she'd get to Buster, wondering whether she'd ever see London or her mother again. Mrs Barker did her best to calm her down and tidily repacked her suitcase for her. A noise outside startled her.

'That sounds like the taxi outside?'

Mrs Barker went to the window to look out. 'No.'

'I'm so nervous,' she said as if the thought had just occurred to her.

'They give you barley sugar, you know,' said her mother comfortingly.

'Who do?' she asked puzzled at the non-sequitur.

'On the plane. For your nerves. When you fly for the first time. I read about it.'

'Oh.'

June stared out of the window as Mrs Barker refolded a pink cardigan. 'Why are you going like this?'

'What else can I do?'

'They might be watching the airport.' Mrs Barker was also prey to all June's uncertainty. She didn't know when, if ever, she would see her daughter and granddaughter again.

'I gotta be with Buster, Mum,' June felt like she was having the same conversation she had had in 1947 when they had first met. 'I'll take the risk.'

'He's only getting a new passport, June. It won't change his character,' Mrs Barker observed tartly.

'And the nose.'

'Still . . .'

Mrs Barker could hold back no longer. The taxi would be there any moment. 'What you going to do in Mexico, anyway? You don't speak Mexican. Where's Nicky going to school? You ain't never been out of this country in your life.'

June snapped the suitcase shut decisively. 'I know all that, Mum. I been thinking of nothing else ever since Buster left.'

'So why are you going? You always said you didn't believe all that rubbish about the dream he had.'

June looked at her mother and all her thoughts seemed to coalesce. She felt a great calm settle over her as she stated firmly, 'I'm married, Mum. And I love him.'

June sat in the departure lounge of Heathrow Airport looking a great deal more attractive and composed than she felt inside. She wore a new top and skirt which she smoothed out continually, partly to keep herself occupied and partly to stop the material creasing, which she found it did very easily.

Nicky was the only young child in the vicinity which made her normal five-year-old behaviour seem exaggeratedly obstreperous. June's hair was newly cut and sprayed with the stiffest lacquer possible. She was determined to create a good impression when she arrived in Zurich. Unfortunately the sophisticated look she was striving for was undercut somewhat by the large rather tatty shopping bag she kept at her feet.

She looked down at her ticket which she held in the name of 'Mrs Pauline Ryan'. She heard the constant refrain of the public address system. 'BEA announce the departure of Flight 916 to Cologne and Hamburg. Would all passengers please proceed to Gate 19.' There was a short pause. June looked again at her ticket which stated 'Flight Departure 0900'. The public address started again.

'This is the final call for the BEA Flight 702 to Zurich. Would all passengers please board through Gate 11.' The clock registered quarter to nine. June remained as if stuck to the seat.

When it got to twenty-past ten June finally plucked up the courage to approach the severe, starched BEA stewardess sitting behind the desk. By now a few loose hairs were starting to peel away from the main beehive hairdo as she tottered over to the desk on her new high heels. Shyly she cleared her throat and waited for the attention to be shown to her.

'Excuse me . . .'

'Yes?'

'When does the flight 900 go?'

'I'm sorry.'

'Flight 900 to Zurich. We're on it.'

'I'm sorry, Madam. We have no Flight no. 900 to Zurich.'

'Oh,' said June meekly and turned to walk back to her seat.

Further reserves of courage were summoned and she approached the desk again and, apologizing, she slid her ticket over the counter.

The stewardess looked up in surprise. 'But, Madam, this flight left on time – at nine o'clock.'

'Oh,' said June, not surprised. 'I was listening to the lady on the loudspeakers. She kept saying about flight numbers. I thought 900 was my flight number.'

'No.' The stewardess softened. 'Nine hundred is the way we say nine o'clock in the morning. It's a twenty-four hour clock. Like in the army.'

'Oh.' June was trying to be helpful but she stood there bemused.

The stewardess checked her schedule. 'I can re-book you on the 1500 hours flight, if you'd like.'

Buster spent a truly miserable morning in the arrivals lounge of Zurich airport. Arriving half an hour early because he didn't want to miss them, he stood discreetly at the back of the hall until forty-five minutes after their flight was supposed to have landed. When June and Nicky didn't emerge from customs he assumed that their false passports had been spotted and impounded.

'Who the hell would want to do that to a mother and a little girl?' he wondered.

His glance started shooting round the lounge. There were at least two possible Interpol characters. One of them at that moment sprinted forward and embraced a very beautiful girl as she pushed her trolley out of the customs shed. Buster mentally wiped him off the danger list. Policemen never showed such emotion in public – even when in disguise. He couldn't go and inquire about Pauline Ryan in case that was exactly what they were waiting for him to do – show up and identify himself as Pauline Ryan's husband. Then the cuffs would be on in seconds and he'd have thirty years to contemplate the naïvety of his actions.

After two hours and with a heavy heart he went back to his hotel in Zurich. What an irony! He'd got the passports, the tickets to Mexico, a new nose (no thanks to that Nazi butcher) and a beautiful (and expensive) diamond necklace for June. He was, metaphorically speaking, inches away from total triumph. But where was his wife?

He lay on his large double bed in the Zurich hotel room where he had spent the past few nights eagerly anticipating June's arrival. He stared at the ceiling, remembering with what fond hopes he had dressed that morning, recalling his thoughts that the next time he undressed it would be with his family around him. If June had been caught now . . . He was as close to despair as he had ever been when the phone at his bedside shrilled.

Just over an hour later he was nervously pacing the foyer of the hotel when Nicky burst in from the street. She flew into his arms and Buster picked her up and flung her into the air. June, a scarf over her head, dark glasses hiding her eyes, followed her daughter to receive an equally warm embrace.

'Where the bleeding hell have you been? You're bleeding seven hours late. I been going crazy.'

But June was too busy critically examining Buster's new nose to answer the question directly. Buster of course became instantly self-conscious and tried to bury it in his hands. June laughed and pulled them away. 'No, Buster. I like it.'

They kissed passionately.

'Did they change anything else while they were there?' she asked saucily. Buster smacked her bottom in reply as Nicky continued to babble on.

'We been on a plane! And I had lots of sweets! And I was sick in the toilet!'

Buster laughed delightedly. He had forgotten how much he'd missed this entertaining gabble.

'Oh, Buster,' said June, tucking herself under his other arm. 'I got the wrong flight ... and you said you'd be at the airport ...'

'I went. I thought I saw Interpol. When you didn't come out of customs I thought they'd got you at passport control. Jesus, I been scared shitless.'

Nicky pulled at his sleeve as they headed for the elevators. 'Is this abroad, Dad? It looks like a hotel to me.'

Later that night June tucked the sleeping Nicky into her bed, turned on the bedside light in case she woke up and tiptoed out into the sitting-room of the suite Buster had taken for them all. Buster smiled as she emerged and timed the popping of the champagne cork to coincide with her shutting of Nicky's bedroom door. He poured two glasses, put down the bottle and went over to embrace his wife. He simply couldn't get enough of her. Buster was on a tremendous high.

Strangely enough, now that the excitement of the journey had worn off, June was experiencing the reverse emotion. Buster was like the Bumpy Dog in Nicky's Noddy books. She wanted to tell him to calm down, give her time and space to adapt, but Buster was such a creature of emotion and instinct she knew it was a pointless request.

'She asleep?' asked Buster expectantly.

'Out like a light,' said June, hoping that Buster

wasn't going to seize this precise moment to rip her clothes off and ravish her on the floor.

As it turned out Buster had other plans in the interim. He gestured towards the champagne as he nuzzled her neck and led her over to the sofa.

'Not surprised, really. Been a hell of a day for both of you. First time out of England, first time on a plane, first time in a Zurich hotel with a sex-starved husband.' He started to bite her neck playfully as they sank onto the sofa together.

June neatly disengaged herself, still troubled by something. Whatever it was, Buster was oblivious of it. 'It's all so hard to take in. I mean, what are we *doing* here, Buster?'

Buster simply delivered his coup de grâce as an answer. He produced a gift-wrapped box from under the coffee table and placed it with exaggerated care next to the two champagne glasses. 'There you go, girl!'

'For me?' asked June unnecessarily.

'You see anyone else here?'

June untied the decorative bow and opened the lid to reveal, first, a jewellery box containing the diamond necklace. 'Oh, Buster! It's gorgeous!' June was genuinely thrilled.

'And the rest . . .' encouraged Buster.

June dipped further into the box and her fingers emerged with three airline tickets and three brand-new British passports, indistinguishable to the naked eye from the real thing.

Buster blew a pretend fanfare. 'De-dah!'

June didn't bother to check the tickets or the passport. It was all happening too quickly for her.

'Mexico,' trilled Buster, unable to restrain himself a moment longer. 'We done it! And look at them passports! They're all right, aren't they? Mind you, they should be. Price we paid for 'em. Still, you get what you pay for – in the end.'

June tried to match Buster's mood of excitement but she was more than ever troubled by the enormity of the decision they had taken to move to Mexico. Now, perhaps for the first time, she realized there could be no turning back. 'Are we all right for money?'

'Yeh. That's why I come to Zurich,' he explained. 'I got the Swiss account working properly now. It goes from here to Nassau and then to Mexico City and finally to Acapulco!'

'How much did you have to fork out, then?' asked June, ever the pragmatist.

Buster shrugged. 'A grand for the courier, two grand for the bank charges. Still, look at them, Juney. That's the good life, that is. What we worked all them years for. The good life.'

Buster's face beamed beatifically. June tried to shine as brightly but her smile was wan and pale in comparison. She was in that hotel room in Zurich because she loved her husband and for no other reason. All the diamond necklaces in the world were no use to her if she didn't have Buster and his love for her. She didn't know what Mexico would bring, but as long as they faced it together she could be happy.

'It's gonna be great,' she said and turned up her mouth to meet his as it crushed down on her.

CHAPTER THIRTEEN

It was everything Buster had dreamed about. As the
NFH Airlines 707 cleared the jutting peaks of the
southern Sierra Madre and they glimpsed the distant
Pacific Ocean, Buster felt he was coming home. His
mind dredged up the payroll snatch at London Airport which he and the rest of Bruce's gang had attempted a few years before and he recalled, almost
with a shudder, the harsh bleak landscape of the
countryside around Heathrow.

Acapulco Airport lay on the fringe of the ocean. As
the wheels touched down Buster felt the cares of the
world drop from his shoulders. Now at last he was
free of Jack Mitchell and the Scotland Yard Robbery
Squad, free of the punitive British Establishment's
desire for revenge, free, maybe, of the constant rip-
off charges of those people who had hidden or
'helped' him to escape. The future was literally
golden. Now he would show June the kind of provider
he was: now he would shrug off the lowly estimations
of his character, the unjustified references to his 'lazi-
ness' that had bedevilled his early brushes with the
legitimate world.

June, on the other hand, was homesick and frightened the minute they stepped off the plane. Like
Buster and Nicky, whom she had cradled on her lap
all the way from Zurich, she was still wearing heavy
European winter clothes more suitable to a cold
spring in Switzerland than the warm tropical heat of
Acapulco. The blast of heat hit them as they climbed
down the mobile staircase from the plane. For a

moment June thought they must have walked behind the engine of the plane which was still hot from the journey. Then the realization hit her that this was the real temperature 'outside'. She had never really liked the heat. Even on the occasional day trip to the beach at Clacton she had consciously sought the shade rather than the sun. Now it felt as though God had left the Universe's oven door open. The prospect that it might always be like this terrified her.

Bruce and his glamorous young blond wife Franny had been able to watch the descent of Buster's plane out of the cloudless blue Mexican sky as they thundered along the open highway towards the airport in their open-top convertible. In previous winters the two of them had spent many months on the French Riviera and they had both taken to life in Acapulco with gusto. Now they looked sleek, tanned and fit in their scanty attire. Bruce was the first to express doubts as to how his friend and his parochial family would adapt to their new surroundings.

'They're not going to know what's hit them at first.'

Franny continued to file and study her nails with deliberation. 'Mmmmm?'

'Buster'll be fine. I don't know about June. It's a bit too far from the Elephant and Castle for her.'

Franny giggled at the incongruity. 'No Bingo and no Mum. What'll she do?'

They smooched gently outside customs, breaking off occasionally to look for Buster, June and Nicky. In the event they were still locked in an embrace when the three of them emerged blinking into the bright sunlight, carrying their battered old suitcases.

Buster inhaled deeply, smiled and turned to his wife. 'Blimey, darling. This is better than a wet Wednesday in Billingsgate market, ain't it?'

Then he spotted Bruce and Franny fondling

each other. 'There they are! Bruce! Hey, Brucey!'

The two men embraced exuberantly. June let the exhausted Nicky off her shoulder and held her by the hand as she walked over to the Reynolds. She shook hands formally with Franny, who admired Nicky without too much enthusiasm, before she was seized in a bear hug by Bruce. She was pleased by the warmth of his welcome, even if still overcome with conflicting emotions. She clambered into the rear of Bruce's convertible. Maybe it wouldn't be so bad after all.

The big American car sped back along the open highway towards the city of Acapulco and the villa in the hills overlooking the bay which Bruce had arranged for Buster to rent. Buster, June and Nicky were all in their different ways responding to the new environment and were unable to match the expansive conversation of the couple in the front.

'Isn't it fab, June?' asked Franny, opting for the safest method of involving her in the conversation.

'Paradise in the sun, that's what it is,' added Buster.

'I ain't never seen nothing as beautiful,' stated June with some conviction.

'Ain't it great the way the airport's right on the beach?' asked Bruce.

Buster's mind again retreated to a grim November day in November 1962 and the Heathrow Airport payroll snatch.

'If we done the London Airport job here, old son, we could've driven off in a speedboat!'

Bruce did not reply. He glanced at Franny. When would Buster realize that they were part of the jet set now – and as such they were above such parochial reminiscences.

Buster failed to grasp the implication of Bruce's silence. He turned to his wife, still drinking in the sights and sounds of Acapulco.

'Look at it, darlin'. All around you. The good life.'
It was the old refrain. Buster started singing, out of
tune, the Gerry and the Pacemakers hit of 1963 'I
Like It'.

Nicky had other things on her mind. 'Can we make
sandpies, Mum?'

'Course you can. Can't she, Buster?'

'She can build sandpies and eat ice cream all day –
every day!'

Buster took Nicky onto his lap and bounced her up
and down. Nicky squealed with pleasure. Their mood
was infectious and in a burst of spontaneous joy all
the adults in the car started to pummel each other in
a physical demonstration of their exuberance.

The villa where Buster was to live with his family
had a swimming pool outside the living-room door
and a terrace overlooking the bay. It meant they had
the famous view of Acapulco from the Elvis Presley
film *Fun in Acapulco* which they had seen in a London
cinema just before they had gone off to rob the train.
For the first time June thought she might be able to
enjoy this foreign place, though her mind drifted constantly to thoughts of her mother. If Buster could
arrange to bring her out, June felt, she would have
everything she needed for happiness.

The next few days were a whirl of activity for June.
With Bruce's help she hired a maid for the villa who
would also help her to look after Nicky, and she found
the local shops where she struggled to purchase enough
food to keep the large American fridge well stocked.

'Dunno why you're buying all this for anyway. We
can eat out every night now,' complained Buster, as
he grudgingly helped her to unpack the groceries.

'We couldn't eat out every night. Besides, look at
this – I've found some steak. Don't it look nice?'

Buster felt the question was rhetorical and ignored it.

June was still terrified by Mexico – by the language and the climate and the sheer impossibility of hopping on a plane and returning to England. Somehow she felt that if it were a two-week holiday and they could stay in a hotel and take snaps and things like that, it wouldn't be so bad. Living as they were in this grand house made it all seem more permanent and more alien.

On the surface, at least, Buster adapted much better, though he too was irritated by the language difficulties and envied Bruce's easy command of it. Bruce might have been talking pidgin Spanish but at least when he ordered coffee he didn't get enchiladas and that was impressive to Buster. He compensated by buying a large white Mercedes which gave him inordinate pleasure.

The following day they all trooped down to the beach at Nicky's shrill request. June, in her methodical way, packed as if they were setting out for a day trip to Brighton on a Bank Holiday when the weather forecast had suggested showers after lunch. Buster almost had to wrestle the small umbrella from her grasp.

'Look at it out there,' he gesticulated. 'Does it look like it's going to rain?'

June looked at the sun blazing fiercely out of a cloudless blue sky. 'You can never tell at the seaside. It might rain later.'

'June, we're in Mexico. It's the summer. It won't rain till the autumn.'

June looked unconvinced. 'You know what the weather's like,' she replied, looking longingly at the umbrella.

The white, white sands of the beautiful Mexican beach stretched in front of them just as Bruce had promised. Buster started salivating at his first sight. It evoked for him the power of the recurring day-dream he had fantasized about back in the urban

133

wasteland of South London. He felt he was coming home. He wondered idly to himself if he'd ever lived in Acapulco in a former existence. He dismissed it. The current existence was just fine.

The English party set themselves up quickly. Buster dug a large hole with Nicky's spade and covered himself up with sand, groaning as if he couldn't move. Nicky flung more sand on him and then sat down as heavily as she could on what she thought was his stomach but which turned out to be his private parts. Buster groaned, this time for real.

June, meanwhile, was tying a straw hat on her head and carefully unfolding the week-old airmail copy of the *Daily Express* Buster had found for her on a news-stand in the foyer of the Acapulco Hilton hotel. It appeared to have been printed on something resembling lavatory paper and June had to spend some time smoothing it out before she could even begin to read an article about the mushrooming of small clothes shops on a street in London called Carnaby Street. June racked her brains. She couldn't for the life of her think where Carnaby Street was. Admittedly she didn't know the West End terribly well but she felt, sitting on a beach in Mexico, as one of the few English people in the vicinity that she ought to know where it was. She thought of the West End, the buses, the shops, the rain, people who talked English and, above all, behaved normally. Tears started to form in her eyes.

Buster, making noises like Frankenstein's monster, slowly withdrew a hand from under the sand and raised it aloft. As if pleased with this liberation he started to stretch his other limbs while Nicky, enjoying the feeling of being chased, shrieked and scampered towards the Ocean. Buster with one last heave, threw aside the blanket of sand that had covered him and which Nicky had patted down with her hands, and, clambering unsteadily to his feet, pounded after his ecstatic daughter.

'Not too rough!' called June weakly as the trail of sand from Buster's footsteps landed on Bruce and Franny who were too preoccupied with each other to notice. Bruce was sensuously massaging suntan lotion up and down his wife's languid body. Franny, her head resting on her outstretched forearms, had her eyes shut and revelled in the touch of her husband's expert fingers as they slid up and down her spine, each downward movement an excuse for his fingers to slip further and further into her bikini pants. Her attempt to dissuade Bruce from this openly erotic manoeuvre sounded to June's ears to be more a grunt of pleasure than dissatisfaction.

'Don't Bruce,' she eventually gasped. 'It's too hot for all that.'

Bruce grinned and smacked her twice firmly on the bottom.

'That too.'

June buried herself still deeper in the *Daily Express*. She didn't normally look at the back pages at home but now the picture of the Queen shaking hands with the English and South African cricketers at Lords seemed of enormous interest. She looked up as Buster returned to her from playing in the sea with Nicky.

'Water's beautiful out there. Clean and everything. Want to go for a dip?'

'No, thank you,' came June's clipped response as she turned her attention to the crossword. Somehow even the fact that the Pacific Ocean was clean June found oddly irritating. She preferred the year-round freezing temperatures of the English Channel even if it was invariably as grey as sewage water.

Buster flopped down heavily on the sand, his pores soaking up the sun's rays. This was the life, the life he had always dreamed about. He heard Bruce's voice behind him. 'Here, Buster. Want some suntan lotion?'

Buster sat up and looked at his friend's gleaming body. He certainly wasn't going to compete directly with the darkly-tanned skin in front of him. He would have to find another way of exhibiting his machismo.

'Nah. Don't need none of that poofy stuff.'

Bruce just grinned, contemplating the prospect of Buster's pallid skin turning a bright shade of red tomorrow. He offered the bottle to June and received another rejection.

'It's all right, Bruce. Me and Buster, we got good skin, we have.'

'Well, you won't have much longer if you don't oil it. This ain't Clacton, you know.'

'Too bleeding right it ain't,' affirmed Buster, slapping the persistent mosquitoes away from his body. 'You don't get sodding flies like these in Clacton.'

'If we was in Clacton,' June speculated aloud, 'we could get some TCP from the chemists.'

'Well, we ain't in bleedin' Clacton,' said Buster irritably as a mosquito took a large bite out of him just below the line of his shorts. 'We're in Paradise in the Sun, remember?' he asked threateningly, as he lay down to bask in the heat and think about the two girls he had seen frolicking in the water next to Nicky. He admired the way they carried themselves so proudly in such skimpy swimwear.

His mind drifted pleasantly in this direction for five minutes while the heat started to draw a layer of sweat all over his body to protect the skin from the sun. He was almost asleep when Nicky arrived, giggling loudly, and deliberately emptied a full bucket of sea water all over him.

'What the fuck?' He sat up spluttering, the anger rising in him instantly. He saw the retreating figure of his daughter and he cooled down just as quickly.

'Very nice that. I could just do with that water. Anyone else fancy a dip?' he asked rhetorically, as he raced Nicky back to the water.

Bruce watched them go and then turned to June, still seemingly immersed in the newspaper.

'Settling in all right?'

'Fine,' came the automatic response. 'Well,' she added, knowing perfectly well that she wasn't settling in at all, and since Bruce was at least in part responsible for her current predicament she thought she might as well not pull any punches, 'it's not quite like I thought it would be.'

'And how did you think it would be?'

'Well,' June lowered the newspaper as she searched for the words that would articulate her deepest feelings, 'You know them big hotels on the front in Brighton – the Grand, the Metropole and that lot . . .'

'Yes.' Bruce was puzzled at this sudden reference to the triumph of Edwardian architecture.

'Well, I thought it would be a bit like that.'

Bruce was almost speechless. He looked around him at the palm trees, the Oasis bar on the beach, the glorious vista of sand, sea, cliff and sky and behind him the mushrooming multi-storey glass and concrete hotels, and beyond the teeming squalour in which the native workers lived. He wondered what possible grounds for comparison June could draw with a seaside resort on the south coast of England.

'What?' he asked dully. 'In Acapulco?'

'Mmmm.' June nodded and returned to her paper.

Bruce sought for the words in his mind to try to impress on June the necessity of conforming to the prevailing conventions in their new environment – but he couldn't find them. He was smart enough to realize that though he and Franny shared the identical situation with June and Buster, that didn't necessarily make them any closer culturally. Bruce was sorry that June, in particular, felt like a fish out of water. Franny didn't help much, it had to be admitted. Franny was younger than June and their interests almost never converged. The younger woman revelled in the sun and the restaurants and the nightclubs and the freshness of the physical relationship she had with Bruce. In contrast June was a restrained, mature woman with interests centred on her home and family. She regarded all Bruce's girl-friends as shallow and vain and thought Bruce picked them only for their obvious physical attributes.

His reverie was interrupted by the arrival of a smartly-dressed waiter from the beach bar with a trayful of cocktails. All the drinks were served in tall, elegant glasses filled with crushed ice and with bits of pineapple and strawberries spilling out over the top. Even Nicky's orange juice was graced with all the trimmings.

'I'll sign for these,' announced Bruce and did so with a flourish as the waiter moved around setting up little white tables on which he placed the glasses.

June took a sip of the Harvey Wallbanger Franny had insisted she tried. She liked it, much to her own surprise. She drank the rest of it quickly and set down the empty glass, luxuriating in the warmth she felt spreading from her throat into the rest of her body. The liquid helped to assuage the thirst that had built up, but after a while she realized she was sweating profusely. She shifted uncomfortably in her chair only to bring her exposed forearm into contact with its hot metal rim. 'Ouch!' She couldn't suppress the inevitable reaction of pain. She looked around for a way of disguising it and spotted Buster still frolicking in the water with Nicky. 'Buster! Your drink's 'ere.' she called.

Bruce and Franny exchanged knowing looks as the harsh Cockney vowels rent the still air of Acapulco.

CHAPTER FOURTEEN

June felt like a prisoner in her own house. She didn't like to go out all that much, certainly not without either Buster or Nicky and preferably not without both of them. Maria did the shopping because she knew where to buy the food and there was almost no point in June going because she couldn't speak the language and made little attempt to learn. She liked to go to the butcher with Maria because she managed to convey her desire for a particular cut of meat, but whenever she let Maria do the cooking, as Buster wanted her to do, the food ended up tasting particularly spicy.

Occasionally Bruce and Franny managed to persuade June to abandon her diet of steak and chips for the evening, and join them in one of Acapulco's excellent restaurants. The day after they had first exposed themselves to the heat of the noonday sun was one such experience. Inevitably both Buster and June had emerged from bed that morning in mutual agony. They compared their shades of crimson and speculated when the pain might eventually start to diminish.

While common sense might have dictated that they decline with thanks Bruce's dinner invitation that evening, Buster persuaded June that it was a matter of pride that they accept. Having set themselves up as proof against the rays of the sun it would be presenting Bruce with hours of fun at his expense if they pulled out now.

The evening turned out to be just as tortured an

affair as they had hoped desperately to avoid. Buster dressed carefully in his best suit and was too embarrassed to change even when Bruce showed up in his most casual Hawaiian shirt with gold jewellery hanging round his wrists and neck. Inevitably the heat in the restaurant soon made Buster even more uncomfortable. He looked at June for permission to loosen his collar. It was granted.

Flushed with this small triumph and tactically overwhelmed by the menu which was in Spanish only, Buster thought he would demonstrate his control of events by taking charge when four Margaritas appeared on the table without their having ordered them.

'What's all this, mate?' demanded Buster aggressively. 'We didn't order any of this clobber. You really got to watch these wankers. Always trying to stick one on you,' he observed about the world in general and Mexican waiters in particular.

The waiter concerned continued to walk quietly away from the table as Franny, revelling in her superior knowledge, explained happily, 'It's all right, Buster. They bring you the cocktails free. It's all part of the service here.'

But Buster was not to be so easily mollified. 'Well, why didn't they say so, then?' he complained, irritated.

Bruce buried his head in the comprehensive wine list as Buster attempted to cover his current embarrassment by picking up the cocktail glass and knocking back its contents in one macho gulp.

'Christ!' he spluttered, 'they've put salt in the bastard.' Buster was outraged. Yet another attempt by dirty foreigners to take advantage of an honest Englishman, he thought. Franny simpered opposite him.

Bruce tried to defuse the situation. 'They're supposed to put salt in the bastard,' he observed calmly. 'The idea is to sip it slowly through the salt rim.'

This helpful piece of advice was received by Buster too late to ameliorate his coughing and spluttering. June tried to help by patting him on the back, forgetting for the moment the excruciating sunburn they were both suffering from.

'Ouch! Get off!' Buster waved his arms about in rage and frustration, the pain in his back now matching the pain at the back of his throat. Angrily he gestured for June to resume her seat.

June did so but her eyes flashed a protest. Buster observed it but ignored the warning signals. Bruce handed the wine list back to the waiter.

'The Pauillac '53,' he commanded. The waiter nodded and retreated. 'It's got a hell of a bouquet,' he added. 'It's from the Mouton-Rothschild Chateau. Franny and me rented a villa near there in the winter of '62. You OK, now, Buster?' he asked.

''Course I am.' The waiter hovered respectfully at the side of the table, pen and pad at the ready. Buster tried to recover lost ground. 'Stupid bleeding waiters. They make me puke.' He looked at the waiter and continued with increasing confidence, secure in the knowledge that the man's command of English would be unable to translate the insult if delivered quickly enough and with a broad enough smile. 'Piss off, you little shitbag. Good job they don't speak no English, eh Bruce? That right, Pancho, eh?'

The waiter looked at Buster gravely, while Bruce and Franny, who had been to the restaurant previously, tried to contain themselves until the riposte had been made.

'Would the Señor care for some McEwan's Export? It isn't chilled but the cellar temperature is quite cool.'

The look on Buster's face was succeeded by a rapid reddening with embarrassment that verged on the puce. June finally came to his rescue as Bruce and Franny burst out laughing, increasing her husband's discomfiture.

'What shall we have to eat, Buster?'

'The tortillas are fab,' interjected Franny quickly. 'Maybe a bit spicy for you two but me and Bruce think they're great, don't we, Bruce?'

Bruce picked up the menu and nodded sagely. 'I can certainly recommend the chilli con carne. As Franny says, maybe a touch spicy for you. You might prefer the guacamole.' He looked up and smiled. 'Don't get that down Lambeth way.'

'Ain't there no meat on this menu then?' asked June plaintively.

'It *is* meat,' said Bruce, attempting to keep the long-suffering whine out of his voice. 'It's just spiced up a bit.'

'I just want some steak and chips,' June stated firmly.

Franny smiled, shaking her expensively-coiffed blond curls with just the degree of superiority calculated to irritate both June and Buster. 'You're in Acapulco, June. You don't have steak and chips in Acapulco.'

By now June was blazing. All the injustices she had suffered since leaving England seemed to focus on this unfulfilled desire for steak and chips. She pushed the table back and rose to her feet.

'I like steak and chips,' she said forcefully, looking straight at Franny. 'It's not often we've been able to afford it. I've got some steak in the fridge. If you want to share it you can come with me.'

And so saying, displaying a rare nerve, June draped her wrap carefully round her bare shoulders and marched out of the restaurant. With an anguished glance at the other two, Buster rose from his seat to cajole her back.

'June? June! Come on, darling!' Buster was suddenly acutely conscious of the social embarrassment his wife was causing him. He was unsure whether to ignore her outburst entirely or show solidarity with her by marching out in a similar huff. Instead he did neither but stood indecisively in the middle of the restaurant watching the disappearing back of his wife. 'June! June!' he called again. But, like Felix, June just kept on walking.

The fiasco in the restaurant set the tone for their stay in Acapulco. Buster, as in London, found himself increasingly torn between his desire to emulate Bruce and Franny and their relaxed style of easy living in the sun, and his instinctive appreciation of the difficulties June was facing. After his first disastrous flirtation with the sun's rays Buster came to share June's dislike for the monotony of the sun's appearance in a cloudless blue sky every morning they woke up.

Occasionally it disappeared and was replaced by threatening rainclouds which dumped an enormous volume of water on the town in the space of an hour or two, but pretty soon the sun was back and it was as if the rain had never been. Buster and June both longed for a really miserable grey day with odd scurries of rain, cold enough to make you shiver through your raincoat. Acapulco was to disappoint them consistently in this.

Ironically the one member of the household to take to Mexico like a duck to water was Nicky. The little girl struck up an instant rapport with their pretty seventeen-year-old maid, Maria, who taught her Spanish and how to swim like a fish. June and Buster were both immensely proud of their daughter's swimming ability but unreasonably disconcerted by her fluency in Spanish. Neither of them made much effort to learn the language since they considered it either irrelevant or too difficult. Although Bruce assured them that children have a natural ear, picking up languages more easily than adults who are more set in their ways, Buster and June both felt that speaking Spanish so easily made Nicky a little less English than they would have liked.

Buster tended to solve the conflict between the various demands imposed by his wife on the one hand and his best friend on the other by drinking heavily and avoiding siding with one or the other. Most afternoons he spent at the private club which Bruce had joined where topless bathing was permitted. Although this was a phenomenon he had already encountered on the French Riviera Bruce never failed to be excited by the exhibition of so much exposed female flesh.

One afternoon on his way to join Bruce, Buster stepped onto the patio to say goodbye to Nicky and Maria when he was accosted by the sight of nearly a dozen local urchins all using his swimming pool. He was about to object to this exploitation by the maid when he observed with pleasure Nicky's delight in the company of the other children. It was really just like playing in the park with neighbourhood kids which she would have been doing had she been home in Lambeth. Buster smiled inwardly as he recognized how he still called Lambeth home, even though their stay in Acapulco might be the equivalent of a life sentence.

'You sure these is all your brothers and sisters, Maria?' he asked querulously.

'Oh, si, Señor', replied the pretty girl easily. 'Except Pedro.' She pointed at a small body whose only visible feature was a shock of dark hair. 'Oh,

144

and Teresa and Rosita.' Two little girls were jumping about in the shallow end, holding hands and jabbering away in what was presumably a Mexican version of 'Ring a Ring o' Roses'.

'Attagirl, Nicky!' called Buster to his daughter as she swam powerfully across the pool in a dignified breaststroke.

'She's like a little fish, ain't she?' he asked admiringly of nobody in particular.

Nicky tried to turn round in midstroke to wave goodbye, swallowed a mouthful of chlorinated water and started to choke. Maria swum quickly to her side. Buster, seeing that he was redundant once more, sloped off back into the living-room.

As Buster entered through the open terrace doors, June sprang out of the kitchen and brought him crashing down onto the couch, tickling him unmercifully until he shrieked.

'June! Stop it! You're tickling!' he complained superfluously.

June remained obdurate. 'Not until you tell me where we're going.'

'Stop it,' cried Buster, attempting with some force to wriggle free of the pernicious hold the tickler retained on him.

'Tell me then,' reiterated his triumphant wife.

'Tell you what?' asked Buster genuinely puzzled.

'Where we're going.'

'When?'

'This afternoon, of course.'

'I'm going to meet Bruce.'

June stopped tickling and sat up abruptly. Buster followed suit.

'I thought,' she said deliberately, 'we was going out together. That's why I let Maria bring all them kids here.'

Buster knew he was in for trouble and he bristled at the unfairness of it all.

'When?' he demanded aggressively. 'When did I say that?'

'Yesterday,' replied June simply.

'I don't remember.' Buster sighed and removed a wad of banknotes folded in half from the back pocket of his lightweight trousers. He licked his thumb and started to peel off half a dozen notes.

'Here,' he proffered, 'go and enjoy yourself. Buy something nice. You know you like to do that. We'll go out together tomorrow. I promise. I'll remember this time, that's for sure,' he added to forestall any riposte by June.

The offer of the money was probably the worst thing Buster could have done. For him it was a measure of how much he loved June. After all, he didn't exactly go around Acapulco thrusting money on any woman who gave him the time of day.

To June the money was symbolic of what she had been reduced to – a chattel who could be bought off in cash. It wasn't the Paradise she had been thinking of when Buster had been talking so persuasively about the delights of Mexico when they had been holed up together in deepest Wraysbury.

'I don't want the money. I got plenty of money.' She got up, hurt, and walked over towards the kitchen –'where I belong,' she thought grimly.

'Yeh, well, let's just hope it stays that way,' muttered Buster, loud enough for June to hear.

At the sound of possible trouble June's ears pricked up. 'What d'you mean? Ain't that ten grand from Switzerland got here yet?' Buster had been speculating why the smooth flow of funds from Zurich to Acapulco via the Bahamas had suddenly developed a snarl-up.

'No. It got lost.'

'Lost? What d'you mean "lost"?' asked June, knowing perfectly well what he meant.

'Just lost. Just that. We got stuffed, O K?' Buster who had simply meant to deflect June's anger at not being able to spend the afternoon with him, was now cross with himself that he had opened a real can of worms.

June, as he had predicted, was now at him like a dog with a bone.

'Who lost it? Where . . .'

'I don't know!' Buster cut in. 'Someone . . . somewhere . . .' he went on, flailing helplessly. 'Look, it'll be all right. Trust me. I'll sort it out.'

'Ten thousand quid!' June's voice took on a new strain of disbelief as she repeated slowly, 'You lost ten thousand quid!'

Buster was now getting very anxious indeed. He shifted uneasily from one leg to another, rattling the change in his pocket as he did so. 'I've told you. Don't worry about the money. We've still got nearly twenty grand left. You just get on with enjoying yourself. Don't wait up. Me and Bruce has got business to talk about.' And with that he slipped gratefully out of the front door and into the fresh air.

Buster felt aggrieved as he drove along the congested streets of Acapulco towards the club. June knew perfectly well he needed to talk to Bruce, to drink with him, to discuss the extraordinary events of their lives, to make plans for the future. Why did she suddenly spring things like that confrontation on him and make him feel guilty? He put his foot down on the accelerator and overtook dangerously on a blind corner. The trailing accompaniment of a chorus of disapproving car horns provided a small measure of compensation. 'Foreign greaseball wankers!' he shouted gaily out of the window.

They met at Bruce's apartment, a short walk from the beachside club. From the balcony of the purpose-built block of luxury apartments Bruce and Franny had a perfect view across the bay. They could also peer down directly on that part of the club where nude, or rather topless, bathing was permitted. To ensure that absolutely nothing was denied him in this respect Bruce had erected a small telescope which he pretended, to those who showed an unhealthy interest in it, he used for the purpose of spotting the ensigns of the different naval vessels which anchored in Acapulco harbour. Alone with Buster, Bruce also wore a pair of binoculars round his neck which he would use to line up the exposed breasts of the various girls laid out before him, before confirming his interest in the telescope.

This afternoon, however, Buster was much less interested in the women than he was in acquainting Bruce with the state of his troubled mind. The conversation with June had stimulated unhealthy thoughts of what they would do when the money ran out.

'We went through it together last night,' he began. 'D'you know we're getting through 250 quid a week out here.' Buster shook his head sorrowfully.

Bruce failed to respond as required, having found a pair of breasts capable of exciting his sometimes jaundiced interest. 'You tried economizing? Christ, look at that pair!'

'You sound like June's mother.'

'Really?' said Bruce, not removing his eyes from the binoculars. 'I didn't know she was fond of big tits. Look, Buster, just look at that girl in the purple pants. Oh, Jesus! It's as good as St Tropez here.'

He passed the field glasses over to Buster who altered the focus before registering surprise. 'Jesus!

They're enormous! It must be the fruit they eat out here,' he added.

Bruce, his eye now clamped to the telescope, indulged in one of his favourite areas of philosophy. 'I love sex. Love it. You don't find tits like that at Margate, my son.'

Buster was alarmed at the turn the conversation was taking. He really needed to talk to Bruce about the money and about problems with June, but Bruce was now in full flow.

'It's a funny thing about sex. Why is it that a pair of knockers 500 yards away is a lot more interesting than Franny's which are currently lying on the bed in there and a lot more available. One of the seven wonders of the world, that is.'

Buster waited for the wind of such speculation to blow itself out before steering the conversation into new areas. 'Bruce, we can't go on like this for ever. Don't you miss it? The planning? The excitement? That was half the fun.'

Bruce stepped back from the telescope with an evident show of reluctance. 'So what do you suggest?'

'There's this bank . . .' began Buster.

'Oh, no!'

'No wait! Wait! It's a. snip. One old guard what picks his nose or he's asleep. No bother . . .'

Bruce shook his head. 'It's dangerous, Buster. We got no contacts out here. What do we do with the money?'

'We spend it, you arsehole. That's why we're taking it. Make a change from old ten-bob notes.'

There was a pause while Bruce tried to tear his mind away from the inviting prospect in front of him to the serious contemplation of armed robbery in a new country.

'I don't like it, Buster,' he pronounced eventually.

'Even if it went off all right, how do we launder it? I mean it'll just tell Interpol where we are. 'Sides,' he added, 'we don't know the language.'

'You do,' cajoled Buster.

'I don't mean just Spanish. I mean the specialist language.'

'I been learning,' proclaimed Buster proudly, confident that Bruce would raise this objection early.

Bruce was duly surprised. 'You?' he smiled.

Buster resented the implication hugely. His hackles rose. 'Yeh,' he said shortly. Very deliberately and in his best Spanish accent as perfected with Maria he said, *'No hay papel higienico en el cuarto de baño.'*

There was a pause. Bruce was impressed. There was no doubt that Buster had been working away at his Spanish. Maybe such a plan was feasible after all. A thought struck him. 'That's very good, Buster. What's it mean?'

The reply came without hesitation. 'There's no toilet paper in the lavatory.'

Bruce retreated to his telescope and delivered himself of a firm opinion. 'You are going to wind up straight back in the slammer.'

Buster was furious at this cursory dismissal of his hard work. 'Piss off, Bruce. You ain't the only one round here with brains, you know. Just 'cause you've gone soft. Ain't no reason I gotta be like that,' he taunted.

Bruce laughed and put his arm round the neck of his old friend, pulling his head down so he could kiss him on top of his little bald patch, knowing how this irritated Buster.

'Come on, Brains, then. We're losing valuable drinking time.'

CHAPTER FIFTEEN

Although the sun had gone down hours ago it was still hot inside the villa. June had dragged an armchair out of the living-room and had placed it on the terrace so that she could continue to knit without feeling stuffy. She enjoyed the mechanics of knitting, the comforting clicking of the needles and the slow transformation of the ball of wool into a practical item of clothing reminded her of evenings spent with her mother, both knitting together while watching television. Of course she realized even at the outset that knitting a large woolly pullover for Buster was not exactly the most useful thing to be doing with her time in the climate that they had experienced so far in Acapulco, but if Buster could enjoy himself indulging with Bruce in some bar June saw no reason why she shouldn't expect a little pleasure herself.

Sitting in her lightweight nightdress, purchased from Marks and Spencer before leaving England, with her feet curled under her, she was just measuring the sleeve of the pullover against her own arm when she heard the sound of a dustbin being knocked over and the ever-increasing decibel level of a famous English rugby song.

'Four-and-twenty virgins came down from
    Inverness,
And when the ball was over there were four
    and twenty less . . .'

Bruce and Buster, though in the highest of spirits, had such terrible voices that they had managed to turn this most raucous of obscene songs into a tuneless funeral dirge. After picking themselves up and finishing in what they regarded as some style, they both stood in silence waiting for a response. It was not forthcoming. The upper-class neighbourhood in which Buster and June had rented their villa was above such bourgeois reactions.

'I think we're in church,' slurred Bruce.

Buster, however, was still thinking about the glories of new conquests. 'Listen, Bruce. If that bank's no good we'll find another and another.'

''Course we will,' agreed Bruce, holding Buster upright and ringing his front-door bell. 'Here y'are. Home. What're you gonna say to June?' he asked as he heard the echoing sound of June's footsteps on the marble tiles inside.

'Don't you worry 'bout her,' proclaimed Buster attempting without success to draw himself up to his full height. 'I can handle her all right.'

June flung open the front door with all the aggravation she could muster, to find her husband with a silly grin on his face and Bruce, who was sobering up rapidly, with a sheepish one.

'Hello, Juney,' shouted Buster jovially. 'Bruce and me, we been having business meetings, ain't we, Bruce?'

Bruce tried hard to look like a man who had been working late at the office. ''S'right, June,' he confirmed. 'Business.'

'Wonderful business, June,' Buster rambled on. 'You wouldn't understand it, of course. Too hard for women, you see . . .'

At this point Bruce, intimidated by June's hostile, cold stare, let go his support of Buster who immediately crashed onto the floor, face first, with a sickening thud.

''S all right, June,' Bruce tried to explain brightly, 'He's just overworked.'

June banged the door in his face. Bruce, feeling his nose rather tenderly, staggered away wondering whether he had brought the car with him earlier that day and if so what he had done with it. Not surprisingly he fell over the dustbin again.

Next day Buster, June and Nicky set off in their new white Mercedes for a day on the beach.

It had not been a good morning. Buster had inevitably woken up with a splitting headache and his mood had not been helped by June's apparent lack of tolerance and understanding. Also, Nicky had woken him up by bouncing on the bed which Buster suspected had been encouraged, at least tacitly, by June. Shouting at Nicky had provoked an instant response from June and thus the morning had continued.

They were dressed for the beach in what they both considered to be the appropriate clothes – a Hawaiian shirt and Bermuda shorts for Buster and a skimpy two-piece bathing costume covered by a garish halter top for June. At least it was discernible 'progress' from their initial adventures in this sphere.

Nicky sat in the back seat, happily unpacking June's shopping bag which was filled with suntan lotion, the latest airmail editions of the *Daily Express*, sandwiches and a thermos flask of cold orange juice. Buster and June, clearly in the middle of yet another row, wore fashionably-outsize sunglasses and stared doggedly straight ahead.

The sound of the slamming car doors caused Buster to wince and mutter under his breath.

'Oh, well,' remarked June with as much venom as she could muster, 'if you're going to be like this we might as well have stayed at home.'

'I've said I'll take you,' spat Buster in reply. 'So I'm taking you.'

'Well, you don't have to be so bad-tempered about it.'

'I ain't bad-tempered,' shouted Buster bad tem-peredly. 'I just got a bleeding headache.'

'Don't you swear at me,' responded June primly, as Nicky discovered the wrapped chocolate biscuit that had been destined for her lunch. She decided she was hungry and began to eat it.

Buster glared sideways at June. What an aggravat-ing woman she could be sometimes. He was sorry he had come back in quite such a drunken state last night but he was suffering more than she because of it, and the very least he felt he could expect from her was an appreciation of the size of his headache this morning.

Buster turned his attention back to the road just in time to see the traffic lights ahead turn to amber. Instinctively he put his foot down hard on the ac-celerator to beat it. Despite the smooth acceleration of the Mercedes he went through on the red to the indignation of the traffic policeman on his wooden rostrum. The man blew his whistle and pointed at Buster who braked violently, hurling his passengers against the nearest piece of car upholstery.

'You idiot, Buster. You went through on the red,' flared June.

'I didn't. It was still amber.'

'So what's he stop you for, then?'

'Leave off, June.'

'Policemen don't stop you just 'cause they don't like your face, you know. He's going to trace the number. You'll see! You'll see if I'm right.'

'Shut up!' yelled Buster. 'Shut up, shut up, shut *up*!'

By this time the policeman with the white gloves was tapping on the window. Buster rolled it down, took off his sunglasses and forced a huge smile out of himself.

'Buenos dias, old son,' he began brightly.

The policeman was in no mood to trade Cockney banter. He gesticulated and shouted while Buster held up his hands in a placatory manner. The abuse continued in a torrent until Buster cottoned on to the logical solution. Assuming that policemen were much the same the world over but that non-European cops were probably more blatant than their more 'sophisticated counterparts' Buster slowly removed his wallet from his back pocket and started to count out a large number of pesos. The torrent of abuse started to slow down and finally stopped when the policeman had decided he had reached the appropriate level of on-the-spot fine.

'Perdone, perdone,' said Buster with a frosty smile. 'No entiendo, no entiendo,' his favourite words of incomprehension.

As the policeman seized the notes and returned to his rostrum where cars from all directions were hooting to attract his attention, Buster sighed and put his wallet back in his pocket. He resented the extortion but even more he worried that June might be right and that he might trace the number.

'I told you,' said June unhelpfully. 'What did I tell you?'

Buster, his head throbbing worse than ever, exploded. 'Shut up, you bag! Just shut your trap!'

June was secretly pleased she had finally won the war of marital attrition. She couldn't help rubbing it in. 'Might as well be in Clacton,' she muttered loudly.

On the beach the two of them began to relax as the warmth of the sun began to dissolve the tensions. Even Buster's headache started to diminish as he lay back and just let his mind wander. June was slowly and painfully counting out shells from Nicky's bucket in Spanish.

'Uno, dos, tres, cuartro, sink-o,' she started laboriously.

'Not sink-o, Mum. It's "thinko". Five's "thinko".'

'Yeh', said June, acknowledging her daughter's superior command of the language, 'That's right, darling.'

As if to confirm the fact, a group of local urchins ran up to Nicky and started jabbering in Spanish to her.

'Can I go and build a sandcastle with them, Mum?' she asked.

'Yes. But stay where I can see you.'

The little girl ran off happily as her mother wondered how a small child learnt a foreign language with a facility that no adult could hope to match. She was proud of Nicky's adaptability, glad that she got on with Maria and the local children so easily but bothered on some unconscious level by the ease with which she relinquished her English persona and adopted a Mexican one. Did that mean she wouldn't be able to change back again? June didn't want to be the mother of a Mexican urchin. It rather frightened her and made the normal paranoia feel worse.

She slapped, almost without thinking, at the hovering mosquitoes. Buster, his eyes open, was looking for a way of starting the conversation and making up to June without conceding too much in emotional territory.

'I'll do that for you, if you like,' he offered smiling. June, equally anxious to resolve matters, grinned back. Buster, responding to a wave of love that washed over him, rolled up to his wife and kissed her passionately.

They lay contentedly together on the warm beach towels.

'Just think of them poor bastards back home,' he

said to her. June thought about them. 'Fog, sleet, car won't start, buses full up, tubes cancelled, can't pay the bills . . .' Buster was enjoying his fantasy of life in London but it bore no relation to June's home thoughts from abroad.

She reminisced nostalgically. 'The pub and the shops and the people and going to the market and taking Nicky to the park . . .'

Their two fantasies completely overlapped. Neither listened much to the other's and what small part they caught they dismissed as insignificant.

It was a good day nevertheless. They seemed to be a family again. Both Buster and June always claimed that this was what they had wanted – the money (or lack of it), Mexico (or England) was irrelevant. As long as they were together, as long as they remained in love with each other it didn't matter what else the world could throw at them.

To celebrate their recovered equanimity they decided to try the new nightclub, the Copacabana that Bruce and Franny had already sampled. They got back into the Mercedes and drove home so that they could change, give Nicky her tea, eat whatever native concoction Maria had cooked in their absence and get ready for their evening on the town. Just to show that the events of the morning were forgiven if not forgotten, Buster drove with deliberate caution, almost like a learner taking his driving test. He indulged in exaggerated waits at road junctions and supplemented the traffic indicator with superfluous hand signals. Approaching the policeman on point duty with whom he had had the confrontation earlier in the day, Buster slowed down well in advance of him and beamed cheerily through the window at the cop. It was with some shock and trepidation that Buster saw the policeman register the presence of his distinctive white Mercedes and climb deliberately off his platform. He sauntered casually over to the car and knocked perfunctorily on the window. Buster rolled it down and swallowing hard, tried to smile. 'Si?'

There followed the inevitable torrent of Spanish which Buster forestalled by turning to his wife who already had the appropriate banknote waiting in her hand. Buster snatched it from her and pressed it into the gloved fist of the policeman. The cop made a passable attempt at a salute and finished with the line that was becoming heard ever more frequently in the American-dominated tourist city. 'Gracias, Señor. Hev a nice day!'

It wasn't so much the flagrant bribery and corruption. After two years of life on the run as one of the most wanted criminals in the world, and still carrying the tag of almost unlimited wealth, Buster was used to the exploitation. What he couldn't work out was whether this new manifestation was a local disease or not. Did his white Mercedes mark him out as just a rich gullible foreigner or had Interpol finally succeeded in identifying his whereabouts?

Buster waited nervously in the car, out of sight of the house, while June and Nicky went inside to make sure Jack Mitchell wasn't sitting on the couch holding a pair of handcuffs. Even though there was no apparent sign of their domestic tranquillity having been disturbed and even though Maria reported nothing unusual during the course of the afternoon, the easy harmony of the day on the beach had been broken. Buster suggested, somewhat diffidently that they give the Copacabana a miss that night but June was seizing on any faltering by Buster in what she considered to be his marital duty and at 9.30 that night, in their best clothes, they set out for the nightclub.

The Copacabana turned out to be a severe disappointment. It was nothing more than an over-priced bar with some half-heartedly 'erotic' dancing going on in the background. June, however, was deter-mined to enjoy herself despite the mood of discontent that had overtaken her husband.

They sat on high stools around the formica-topped bar which, apart from the signs in Spanish, could just as well be somewhere in Soho, Buster thought mourn-fully. June, wearing the shortest skirt he had ever seen her try out in public, looked around her approvingly, trying hard to have the fun she believed her husband had when he was with Bruce. 'It's very nice here, ain't it, Buster?'

'It's a scream.'

'I wish Mum was here. She'd like it.' It was June's dearest wish that her mother could enjoy some of the fruits of their 'success'.

Buster didn't share this dream. He jerked his head in the direction of the 'dancing' girl, who in reality was little more than a glorified stripper. 'I think that's her over there.'

June bristled. 'Buster!'

A small, swarthy man with a thick black moustache, much favoured by the local male population, ap-proached from the other end of the bar and, wiping the pool of liquid in front of them, asked brightly in purest Cockney, 'What'll it be, folks?'

'I'll have a straight Scotch and my sister here'll have a port and lemon,' replied Buster immediately.

The barman looked at them both steadily, a large smile peeping out from underneath the moustache and his eyes twinkling with anticipated pleasure.

'Now, that's what I like to hear!'

Buster frowned. 'Eh?'

'Where you two from?'

Buster decided to play stupid. He could immediately see this wasn't a conversation to be encouraged.

'I recognize that accent,' commented the barman jovially. 'You're from South London, ain't you?'

Buster found this one difficult to deny. 'Yeh. Sort of.'

'I'm from Streatham,' boasted the barman proudly. 'Where you from?'

June seized on the possibility of a friend. 'Oh, we're from round Kennington way,' she said eagerly.

'No shit? Or "far out" as they say a lot round here. You know there's a shop in the Hilton Hotel foyer where you can get McEwan's Export. It's in tins of course, but it's not bad.'

'Oh, I know that place,' responded June. 'You can get Weetabix and Sugar Puffs there too. And Jusoda.'

'Wouldn't know about that.'

'Ain't it expensive, though? I mean, who'd pay nearly fifteen bob for a packet of breakfast cereal, eh? Used to be three and ninepence.' June could have this sort of conversation all night.

Buster interjected as an American at the far end raised his hand and flashed a twenty-dollar bill at the barman who studiously ignored him.

'I think that fella wants serving down there,' said Buster pointedly.

'He can wait. Yank!' observed the barman without feeling. He smiled at June. 'How long you been stuck in Paradise, then?'

'Oh, we're just tourists,' said June, following the line laid down by Buster. 'Doing the sights. You know.'

'Package trip is it?'

'You could say that,' interjected Buster, anxious

not to arouse the nosy barman's suspicions with any-thing in the way of facts, true or false. 'Look, ain't you going to serve that geezer?'

By now the barman had poured himself a Jack Daniels and was staring hard at Buster.

'I seen you before, mate. I know, you ever go drink-ing in the Crown and Garter on the Old Kent Road?'

'Nah. Not me,' said Buster shortly. This was just what he didn't want to hear. 'Look, that bloke's get-ting really pissed off with you.'

'The Mitre in Lambeth?' continued the barman, determined to solve the mystery.

'Only sometimes.'

'I seen you. I know I seen you somewhere. Never forget a face, me. My business it is.' He wandered thoughtfully to the other end of the bar to placate the unquiet American.

Buster took out his wallet hurriedly. 'You stupid berk,' he complained to June. 'What you want to go chatting him up for?'

'I wasn't chatting him up,' protested June indig-nantly.

'He recognizes me, that bloke,' said Buster, fumbl-ing for his change. 'I'm sure he does. Come on, let's go.' He started to pull June off her bar stool.

'Buster, don't!' she reacted, wrenching her arm away from his grip.

'Oh, hello again,' she smiled winningly at the re-turning barman.

'You ever been in the Duck and Feathers in Cam-berwell?'

'Look, we've got some friends we've got to meet.' Buster placed the money in a saucer and added an over-generous tip.

The barman put the money in the till and pocketed the tip without a word of response. Instead he pursued the line of social affability that was his professional trademark. 'Listen, my bird's here too. We could go out for a foursome on my night off. That's usually Thursday, sometimes Mondays. What d'you say?'

'Oh, that would be lovely,' enthused June.

'Hey, man, great, far out.' He paused for a moment and the frown returned to his face. 'It's funny but I could *swear* I seen you before somewhere.'

Buster took a better grip on June's arm. 'See you later then,' he called as he and his reluctant wife headed for the exit.

'Right, mate,' called the barman. As Buster's retreating back was about to disappear through the door a look of ecstacy passed over his features.

'I've got it,' he shouted in a voice that Archimedes could scarcely have bettered when scrambling out of the bath. 'The Elephant and Castle. The Three Kings? Am I right? The Three Kings in the Elephant and Castle?' he called to Buster as he dragged June through the front door and into the night to look for the car.

But answer came there none – except from an American customer who had followed the verbal interplay with interest.

'What is this?' he wondered aloud. 'A quiz show?'

CHAPTER SIXTEEN

The black police Humber Super Snipe purred up Wood Lane from Shepherd's Bush Green and turned left into the entrance of the new BBC Television Centre. It came to a dead stop in front of the lowered barrier. A BBC person emerged from the BBC hut and spoke sharply to the driver as if to indicate that not all his airs and graces and fancy motor-car would furnish him with one of the few prized parking places at Television Centre. Though the building had only been open for a few years it was already clear that the architects had failed to predict accurately the numbers of television people who wanted to bring their own cars to work. The BBC had gone to great pains to acquire a site opposite the White City tube station. Now it would appear that the rising tide of working-class affluence in the Britain of Harold Wilson was even permeating the traditionally underpaid echelons of the BBC.

Mitchell handed Sergeant Chalmers his letter of invitation from the producer of a television programme. 'We're here to meet the bloke who makes *The Global Village* programme,' Chalmers explained to the security guard.

The guard looked at the letter and then turned it over, apparently spending as much time examining the rear of the paper on which nothing was written at all. He appeared unimpressed by the text. 'Sorry. You can't park here with this. More than my job's worth.'

'We're supposed to be at this meeting five minutes ago.'

'Sorry. More than my job's worth,' he repeated with deadening monotony.

Mitchell saw a chink of light. 'All right if we get out here and my driver picks us up after the meeting?'

The bastion of the BBC considered. 'I'll have to make a phone call,' he decided.

Jeremy Pownall, the fashionably dressed, mop-haired producer of *The Global Village*, nibbled a pink wafer biscuit and gesticulated in the direction of the large map of the world behind him.

'It's the biggest telecast ever done. It'll make Richard Dimbleby standing on Goonhilly Downs look like that white-haired old geezer singing "Abide with Me" before the Cup Final.'

Mitchell and Chalmers exchanged glances of total incomprehension. They were seriously out of their depth here.

'The Beatles have agreed in principle to appear but we're having a small problem with Mr Epstein, their manager, so the contract's not signed yet.'

This time it was the turn of the other BBC executives to exchange smiles as they recognised a bullshitter when they saw one. Pownall pressed on regardless.

'I've asked Inspector Mitchell of the Yard to come here today because I've come up with a lulu of an idea. C-BBC 1 thinks so as well and MD Tel has already given the go-ahead. Inspector Mitchell the floor's all yours.'

Mitchell cleared his throat noisily. 'Thank you, Mr Powell. Over two years ago, you will recall, gentlemen, the Great Train Robbers made off with two and a half million pounds from the Royal Mail Train . . .'

'. . . I meant to ask you Inspector,' interjected Pownall, 'how much of that did you ever recover?'

'Oh, Buster,' she gasped, 'this is great, ain't it?' She struggled to sit up to find her romantic husband with his head over the side being violently sick into the Pacific Ocean.

An hour later Buster lay stretched out in the sun, his wife cradling his head as it nestled in her lap. Somewhere out there the sun was setting, turning the Gulf of Mexico a stunning shade of deep pink. Stretched out before them in a 360–degree panorama lay the sort of sights that had impelled Magellan and Vasco da Gama to set out on their journeys of epic adventure. June and Buster lay wrapped entirely in concentrating on the immediate problems of Buster's well-being.

'You're a stupid berk, ain't you, Buster?' sighed June, her fingers smoothing his thin hair.

Buster's reply was indistinguishable.

'What are you?' repeated June tenderly.

'A stupid berk,' groaned Buster in the same cadence.

'I don't know why I love you, you know.'

'Me neither.'

'I wish we was in Battersea Park,' began June, as Buster raised his eyebrows in surprise at the apparent non-sequitur. 'We could go on the lake there, and have tea and an ice cream at that little café, then we could lie on the grass and then we could buy fish and chips for tea and go to the Odeon or maybe up West some-where.'

The reverie acted like a sexual fantasy for June. 'It's only 'cause I love you so much I'm staying here, you know,' she pointed out.

'I know, but . . .'

'I wish we could go back.'

June stopped Buster's protest with a kiss. Buster became instantly aroused. He had always responded

169

naturally to June's occasional advances. They lay comfortably on the floor of the boat, their hands searching for each other, giving and offering the comfort they both needed so badly. The Mexican skipper observed the frolics laid out for his delectation beneath him. His eyes widened in surprise. This too required little in the way of translation. His sole surprise was the reputation the English had always carried as being unromantic and sexually unresponsive. He would have to revise his national stereotypes.

It was after lunch on Sunday that Buster sprang the news. June had gone to considerable trouble to find a cut of beef that she was familiar with so that the Sunday roast would turn out all right but, predictably, had received no thanks at all from her husband or their guests. Her sole satisfaction had come from talking slowly in English to Maria and showing her how to cook a proper English roast beef.

Now she was suddenly confronted with the stark proposal of crossing the line from being an accessory after the fact to a conspirator. Whereas Franny was looking forward to executing the plan as devised, June had no such anticipation.

'Come on, Juney,' coaxed Buster. 'It'll be a doddle!'

'That's right,' added Franny. 'It'll just be a bit of a giggle, that's all.'

'What makes you think it'll be that much of a diversion anyway?'

'Oh, come on, June! Ain't you seen them on the balcony looking at the girls?'

'That just helps us concentrate,' protested Bruce.

'Anything with naked women in it and you're happy,' observed Franny tartly. Turning to June she added in a kinder voice, 'We should really help the boys when they need us.'

June sat there, squirming and unhappy. She didn't want to let Buster down in front of the others, knowing how proud he was, but she really didn't want to get mixed up in anything like what was being suggested. Fortunately at that precise moment Nicky managed to upset a beaker of dirty paint water and June seized the chance to rush from the table to clear it up. As she disappeared into the kitchen Franny brought up their contingency plan.

'She ain't going to do it. You can see that. It'll have to be Rosita.'

'Oh, come on,' Buster said dismissively, 'She's just a little tart. She'd be hopeless on a job.'

'At least she'd be willing,' mused Bruce. 'More than we can say about someone else.'

A grin crossed Bruce's face as he thought a little more about Rosita and the effect the girl might have on his stolid friend. Both Bruce and Franny had already discussed the potentially explosive effect on Buster the lissome young Mexican girl might have.

Buster resented their conspiratorial look and called out to the kitchen, 'June, darling, you'll have to do it. Otherwise these two bastards here is going to fix me up with some nineteen-year-old dolly bird.'

June emerged from the kitchen holding a wet sponge. She looked Buster straight in the eye as she spoke quietly but firmly. 'If that's what you want, go right ahead.'

The bank stood on the main street of a small town about half way between Acapulco and La Orilla. At 10.30 on a Thursday morning it was as quiet and sleepy as it was at the same time every morning, or if the truth be known, at nearly every other time during the day. In the carefully stolen car they had chosen for the occasion Buster sat in the rear with the attractive

Rosita, formerly a maid at the Beach Club where she had first been noticed by Bruce and Buster. He looked at her occasionally while trying to summon up the right sort of concentration necessary for the successful execution of the plan in hand.

Rosita meanwhile chatted to Franny and to anyone who would listen in a charming mixture of fractured English and incomprehensible Spanish. She laughed at her own joke and smiled brightly at Buster who smiled weakly back again, trying hard not to look at her chest which, like the car, had been chosen specially for the occasion and which appeared to Buster to be spilling out everywhere.

The car drove up and parked outside the small bank whose exterior Buster had first seen in the photographs handed him so casually by Bruce in the Hilton coffee shop a month before. Like all their English jobs Bruce and Buster had done a number of dress rehearsals, leaving as little to chance as possible, particularly as they had two amateurs on the operation this time. Bruce thought briefly of the highly-trained, skilled operators who had gathered at Leatherslade Farm and then dismissed the thought from his mind. No good thinking about them. They couldn't help. They were in a variety of English prisons, invariably in the maximum security wings.

At 11.10 a van drew up outside the bank and parked. Out of it got two somewhat lethargic guards who wandered casually into the bank. They appeared to have guns but no real sense of vocation. Bruce and Buster followed them inside.

In the dark hall of the bank Franny and Rosita were queuing for the services of the sole teller. Bruce and Buster joined the line behind them. As Bruce saw the first guard emerge from the inner recesses of the bank he nodded briefly at Franny who immediately burst into a torrent of totally convincing hysterical invective. Rosita responded in kind in Spanish and within seconds the two young women were physically grappling with each other. They crashed through the onlookers, over a table and onto the floor, tearing each other's clothes off as they did so.

The sound of ripping bodices was followed, to the astonishment of the onlookers, by the exposure of bare flesh. The concentration of bank customers and employees alike on the two women was total. This sort of free entertainment rarely reached a small town like theirs.

Meanwhile Buster and Bruce had taken advantage of the confusion to find their way unobserved into the back of the bank where the guards were emerging to see just what the excitement was all about.

With an unspoken understanding born of years of working together in just such a situation, the two Englishmen chose a guard each and clubbed him to the floor swiftly and with the minimum fuss. As Franny and Rosita rose and pummelled each other towards the open door, Bruce and Buster slipped out with the four bags of cash into the alleyway at the rear of the bank where their car had been deliberately parked. They unlocked the two nearside doors as the engine roared into life. With a squeal of burning rubber Bruce wrenched the car at high speed round two corners and screeched to a stop by the pavement at the point where Franny and Rosita, still encouraged by the crowd, were seemingly scratching each other's eyes out. As the car stopped Rosita and Franny scrambled to their feet. Franny got into the front passenger seat and Rosita into the rear where Buster was holding the door open for her. The doors slammed and the car set off at high speed for Acapulco. The crowd sighed with regret that their entertainment had been so cruelly taken from them. They dispersed unwillingly, half hoping that the two crazy women would reappear and resume their entertaining wrestling match. It was nearly ten minutes later that it was discovered that a robbery had taken place.

The car weaved drunkenly all over the road as the sounds of laughter and celebration rent the still desert air. Four bags of cash didn't compare in any way with the 120 mailsacks they had once removed from the Glasgow–London Royal Mail train but the satisfaction was just as tangible. Bruce and Buster felt a sense of professional pride that they had planned and pulled off a job in a foreign country, barely speaking the language. The two women were high on excitement and adrenalin which the men had often known. Buster ripped open the first of the bags and shook the banknotes all over his pretty companion in crime. She laughed as she picked them out of her cleavage but Buster's face had fallen.

'Pesos! Fucking pesos!'

Quickly he opened the other three bags. Their contents were identical.

'Is no dollar?' asked Rosita naïvely.

Bruce braked sharply and turned round to examine the depth of the problem.

'Shit!'

'I thought you said . . .' began Buster.

'It's always dollars. Always. I checked.'

'Well, it wasn't this time, was it, genius? You ain't the only one with brains round here.'

Bruce was angry. He didn't like things going wrong like this. 'I suppose we should've sent you in to ask for the loot in Spanish. Right little performance that would have been.'

'That's enough, boys.' Franny's voice broke in sharply. This wasn't the time to fall out. 'It's still money ain't it? I mean, we can still spend it.'

The men said nothing. Their silence was assent to the truth of the statement, but the wind had been knocked out of their sails. Rosita didn't seem to mind. It had been a thoroughly enjoyable day as far as she was concerned and even though her share was going to be in pesos rather than the more highly-prized dollars, she would still be able to afford that gorgeous plum-coloured cocktail dress with the daringly high hemline she had been admiring for the past few weeks in the window of Acapulco's top department store.

While Rosita warmed to the prospect of the looks of appreciation she was going to attract from the men, Buster recalled that special moment of euphoria when they had poured the money over the kitchen table in Leatherslade Farm. Somehow, despite evading the clutches of the police for over two years and living the good life in the swinging tropical resort of Acapulco, it seemed to him that his life had reached its summit on a cold morning in August in a damp farmhouse in the Buckinghamshire countryside.

CHAPTER SEVENTEEN

It was never discovered how Mitchell and Chalmers had managed to find their way onto the floor of Studio Six just a minute or so before the BBC went on air with their live transmission of the British contribution to *The Global Village*. The famous presenter was being touched up by make-up as the harassed director in the production gallery shouted vital instructions picked up by the earpiece he was discreetly wearing. The cameramen were checking their lenses, their trackers were checking the cables, ensuring that when the cameras moved noiselessly over the studio floor they didn't cross their cables.

Mitchell and Chalmers stood transfixed in front of a huge blown-up photograph of Buster Edwards and Bruce Reynolds. 'That's very good isn't it, Chalmers?' said Mitchell admiringly.

'Yes, it is,' agreed Chalmers. 'Except of course they won't neither of them look anything like that any more, you realize.'

'Best we can do,' muttered Mitchell.

'Three minutes to on-air, Studio,' yelled a floor manager hoarsely. He'd been doing a lot of shouting recently.

Up in the production gallery where the gabble on the earphones originated, the frustrated director was bellowing down the talkback – an unnecessary act since the microphone was inches from his face and the earphones were all wedged firmly on the ears of the appropriate technicians. He turned to his production assistant who had the sort of temperament that would have enabled her to have remained calm on the deck of the *Titanic* as it sank beneath the Atlantic.

'Is that film in telecine yet, Elaine?'

'Yes, Gordon.'

'Have you checked?'

'Yes, Gordon.' She looked at her stopwatch and then at the remorselessly moving second-hand on the clock in the gallery to the right of the bank of monitors. She leaned forward and spoke quietly into the talkback. 'One minute to transmission.'

The director looked at her with scepticism. It was all very well for her to sit there exuding competence and calm but it wouldn't be her neck on the line if the screens went blank across the whole world.

'Check again,' he snapped at her.

As Elaine talked soothingly to telecine, the screens in the production gallery, far from going blank, showed four pictures of Detective Inspector Mitchell and Detective Sergeant Chalmers as they strolled casually across the back of the famous presenter's chair. Even the phlegmatic Elaine was momentarily alarmed. The director's anger went off the register.

'Ted!!' he screamed at the floor manager, 'who the fuck is that? Who are they? Get the fuck off my show!'

'Thirty seconds to transmission,' intoned Elaine.

'I'll kill them,' yelled the director. 'I will, I'll kill them!'

On the floor of the studio the floor manager, hysteria pouring out of his ears, strode swiftly to confront the two policemen.

'Who are you?'

Mitchell informed him and produced his warrant card. 'We're responsible for the Great Train Robbers bit.'

'Ah,' replied the floor manager with the instant grasp of the situation that had so endeared him to Elaine on location. 'If you go up that iron staircase right now you can be the director's personal guests in the gallery.'

'Fifteen seconds, Studio,' he shouted, relaying his beloved's latest words in his ear.

As Chalmers and Mitchell took their seats in the gallery they saw the famous, handsome presenter stare directly at the camera and intone, 'This is the British Broadcasting Corporation in London. As part of the international telecast *The Global Village*, broadcasting live to 300 million people around the world, we present 'Salute from London'.

Two of the 300 million people were lying in bed in Acapulco. One of them was eagerly scanning the football results for news of Charlton Athletic, the other was watching the international broadcast and waiting with anticipation for the British contribution. When the ubiquitous Spanish voice was replaced by the mellow tones of the BBC June sat bolt upright in bed, scarcely daring to miss a second of the impending pleasure. As the images of London flashed past on the screen, accompanied by the stirring 'Knightsbridge March' by Eric Coates, June nudged Buster in high excitement. 'Look, Buster, it's London. Look! You can see Big Ben!'

Buster lowered the paper and abandoned his contemplation of the Football League tables for a moment.

'Terrific,' he exclaimed in a bored voice as a picture of Marble Arch dissolved into one of Piccadilly Circus.

'Look, Buster, that's Buckingham Palace and that's Tower Bridge! Oh, look, there's Harrods!'

June was still hugging herself as the opening montage finished and dissolved to a shot of the famous presenter sitting at his desk in front of the large pictures of Buster and Bruce.

'Nearly three years ago these two men were the ringleaders in a massive two and a half million pound train robbery. Ronald 'Buster' Edwards and Bruce Reynolds are the only members of the gang to evade arrest and trial.'

The newspaper dropped from Buster's nerveless fingers as he listened with increasing dismay to the impassioned tones of the famous presenter.

'We would like to take the opportunity of this unique moment in broadcasting history to ask you, the television viewers of the whole world – have you seen these men? Somewhere these two men and their wives are in hiding. There is still a huge reward of £50,000 out for anyone giving information leading to their arrest . . .'

June was the first to snap out of the trance they both seemed held in. 'Turn it off!'

'What?' said Buster, still dazed.

'Turn it off! Turn it off now!'

Buster scrambled out of bed and switched off the set. He stood, naked and indecisive, in the middle of the bedroom.

'Buster,' said June slowly, 'That was the BBC.'

'Yeh, well,' he replied with a lightness he didn't truly feel, 'I never liked the BBC much anyway. Me, I always liked the adverts, meself.'

June shook her head, as if to clear the daze that surrounded it. 'Stop it. Stop joking. All over the world they seen that. Ain't nowhere we can go now someone won't recognize us. The whole world's against us, Buster.'

Buster thought about the truth of June's assertion and accepted it. 'Blimey!' he said with feeling.

*

It was the week before Christmas when Mitchell finally accepted that the publicity generated by the international telecast was not going to produce either Buster or Bruce. He sat reading endless reports of false sightings from Blackburn to Bangkok as Chalmers entered with news of yet another dead-end. Mitchell banged his file shut and swore loudly.

'Jesus Christ! Where the hell *are* they? Every police force in the world looking for them and not a trace of them!'

'They must be paying fantastic protection money. They're bound to break cover soon.'

Mitchell got up and wandered past the desultory line of Christmas cards on the mantelpiece and looked out across the Embankment. He couldn't help but recall the conversation he had had with Dick Poyser when he had received the first grudging intimation of his promotion. He remembered Poyser's uncharacteristic bitterness at how his career had been abruptly terminated by the failure to capture the last two Train Robbers.

'When's soon? Reynolds and Edwards, they did for for old Poyser. I'm not going the same way.'

Chalmers could almost feel the frustration. He offered the only known remedy. 'Shall we go for a drink, sir? Seeing as it's nearly Christmas?'

Christmas in Acapulco was a very different affair. The sun continued to shine out of a cloudless blue sky and Christmas dinner took place on the patio by the swimming pool with the view of the bay in the background. The living-room was knee-deep in wrapping paper and opened boxes, with the exiles attempting to compensate for not being in England by a lavish display of conspicuous consumption.

At the conclusion of the meal everyone was

pleasantly lubricated with alcohol. The men had treated themselves to an enormous Havana cigar each, as they sat back in their chairs contemplating the difference between Christmas in South London and Christmas in Acapulco.

'Not the same without brandy sauce,' declared Buster, puffing away contentedly.

'Can't get brandy sauce,' stated June firmly as she started to clear the dishes away. 'We tried everywhere.'

Buster put his feet up on June's vacated chair and expounded his philosophy. 'What's the point of Christmas without Christmas pudding and brandy sauce?' he asked rhetorically.

'And proper turkey like you get in MacFisheries,' added Franny, whose own memories of Christmas at home were slightly befuddled.

'And the Queen,' said June as she disappeared with a full load of dishes into the kitchen.

Buster rose unsteadily to his feet and raised his glass solemnly. 'The Queen! God Bless Her Majesty!'

Bruce and Franny climbed to their feet and joined in the Loyal Toast with due reverence.

'Only one thing wrong with Her Majesty,' concluded Buster.

'What's that, then?' asked Franny obligingly.

'Her bleeding prisons!' yelled Buster to a chorus of laughter and applause.

June returned to the table and sat down again, shooting Franny a glance that, had the younger woman bothered to interpret it, would have had something to do with helping to clear the table. 'Wish we was back in England for all this,' she said, waving her right arm vaguely in the direction of the panoramic view of the bay.

'Come on, June,' cajoled Bruce. 'Where else could you celebrate Christmas better than here? Look at it. Sea and blue sky and sun and the rest of it,' he concluded lamely.

'London,' answered June immediately. 'With snow and ice and fog and the boozer.'

Buster was now drunk enough to switch sides and support his wife. 'Yeh. And decent snout and no flies and people what talk the Queen's English.'

The end of his tirade coincided with a splutter from Nicky who a minute ago had been contentedly stuffing Christmas cake into her mouth. Buster turned to thump her jovially on the back when he noticed that her face was bright red.

'Mama!' called Nicky plaintively as she started to vomit over the table. The Christmas spirit left the party abruptly.

Later that night while Buster tried for the umpteenth time to get the doctor on the phone, Nicky lay in bed tossing and turning with fever. June sat anxiously by her side and wiped the sweat away with a face flannel dipped in cold water, but the little girl continued to moan and babble. June had stripped the bedclothes off and given her some child aspirin but nothing seemed able to bring down the fever.

'Try to get some sleep, precious.'

'Can't,' moaned Nicky.

'If you get some sleep the fever'll break.'

'I want the doctor,' came the plaintive cry.

June rose and went into the living-room where Buster was banging the receiver down in frustration.

'Where is he?'

'Still no answer. Must have gone away for Christmas.'

'We've got to get a doctor, Buster,' said June,

unable to keep the note of anxiety out of her voice. 'Her temperature's gone up to 104.'

'Oh, kids often run high temperatures,' replied Buster airily. 'That don't mean nothing.'

Buster's ignorance masquerading as knowledge blew a fuse in June. 'What the blazes do you know about it? She could be dying for all you know.'

'Don't get hysterical, June,' said Buster soothingly. 'In a crisis you always panic.'

'I'm not panicking,' shouted June, 'but that child needs a doctor quick. I don't know what's wrong with her and neither do you!'

Buster agreed. 'We'll take her down to casualty.'

'We don't speak the language,' moaned June softly, her mind already imaging the worst possible developments. 'We should never have brought her to this Godforsaken place!'

By the time they arrived in the main waiting room of the hospital Nicky had fallen into a troubled sleep. Buster and June, the latter of whom at least was used to the standard waiting time in any normal British National Health Service hospital, were both horrified to be confronted by the sight of a large hall crammed full of silently-waiting sick or injured Mexicans. Though the majority of them were sitting in stoic silence, the lack of conversational buzz meant that the air seemed full of cries of pain.

The two little foreigners felt themselves to be overwhelmed.

Suddenly Buster spotted a doctor in a frayed white coat examining an old lady. Buster, holding Nicky in his arms, marched over to him. June hurried along in his wake.

'We want to see the Head Honcho,' announced Buster.

The doctor, who was bandaging a painfully wealed

arm that looked as though it had been badly burned, concentrated on the job in hand and ignored Buster's aggressive demand.

'I got a sick child here. Are you listening, woppo?'

'Buster, don't,' begged June, tugging at his arm.

'Leave off, June,' he said, shaking his arm free. 'Look, look, stupido! This little girl's ill. Ain't you going to do something?'

The doctor finished the bandaging and turned to Buster. He looked as though he hadn't been to bed for days. 'Señor, all these people are also ill. You must wait.'

'Wait!' screeched Buster. 'How can we wait? Feel her! She's wet through! She could be dead before you get to her.'

As if on cue Nicky woke up and started to cry. The pain and the fever seemed to have taken possession of her again. The crying inflamed Buster who followed the doctor to his next patient almost pointing Nicky at him like a gun.

'Listen to her, you stupid wop! Listen!'

The doctor ignored the insult and the request, and continued his ministrations to the patient. June grabbed the sobbing Nicky out of Buster's arms.

'Christ, Buster!' Just get out of here. Give me Nicky and just go away.'

'Don't be stupid,' protested Buster.

'I ain't being stupid. It's bad enough to have Nicky ill in this filthy place. Don't you go upsetting the doctor as well.'

'Oh, yeh,' complained Buster, 'I might have known it was all my fault. Who did I do it all for, if it weren't you two? Eh? You was the one what was always on about the good life an' all that.'

'Not here, Buster,' sighed June. 'Can't you see? Even after all this time? It ain't worth a tin of beans out here!'

'Well, what the fuck am I supposed to do about it then?'

Buster was, by turns, angry, confused and worried. June was obviously the one who was going to have to cope in the nightmare of the hospital. She became acutely aware of everyone in the waiting hall regarding the rowing English couple with fascination. Wearily she turned back to her husband.

'Go back to the house, Buster. Ain't nothing you can do for us out here.'

'She's my daughter, ain't she?' argued Buster. 'I ain't leaving.'

Buster's anger stemmed from his inability to do anything to help in this situation. An apology, however, was beyond him, mostly because he felt he hadn't done anything wrong. He sat down grumpily on an overcrowded bench, squirming his body into the Mexicans on either side to make room for his wife to sit beside him. June, however, pointedly didn't want anything to do with him and went to sit on the opposite bench. She cradled Nicky, wiping her fevered brow, and talked soothingly to her. Buster leaned forward and shouted past the blank, uncomprehending Mexican faces, 'I done it all for you, you know! Ungrateful cow!'

At 7.05 the following morning Buster awoke to find himself pressed up against an old garage mechanic with psoriasis. He rubbed the sleep out of his eyes and looked for June and Nicky. The whole waiting area had thinned out dramatically since the previous night and there was a bright young nurse in a crisp starched uniform on duty at the previously untenanted desk. Buster ran over to her. 'My daughter! Where is she? Where's my wife?'

The nurse's command of English was not as great

as the doctor's had been and she started to explain in Spanish that she couldn't understand what he wanted, but Buster, hearing the first words of the now hated Spanish language, swore loudly and started to run in the direction of where he thought the wards would be.

Bouncing off the occasional trolley and ignoring the shouted questions, Buster stuck his head into room after room until he saw, to his infinite relief, the welcoming sight of Nicky sitting up in bed as bright as a button. He was so pleased to see them, so delighted to discover that the nightmare had a happy ending after all, that he totally failed to perceive the grim stare emanating from June who sat in an upright chair on the other side of the bed.

The doctor, who now looked as though he had been without sleep for a week, smiled warmly at Buster, ignoring the previous night's rudeness and hostility.

'Buenos dias, Señor. Your little Nicky, she plays a good game. Tic-tac-toe they call it, no?'

'No,' croaked Buster hoarsely, 'Noughts and crosses we call it. Where did you take her to? Why didn't you wake me?'

'She say her mama always do it.'

'Eh?' asked Buster, puzzled.

The doctor put his hand in the pocket of his white coat and brought out three small coins.

'In the Christmas cake,' he explained. 'They do not taste so good. She have food poisoning. We pump her stomach. We get rich! Forty pesos!'

The doctor smiled as Buster laughed, with more than a trace of hysteria. June, however, remained sitting in stony-faced silence.

They went home, exhausted and grateful for the minor nature of the complaint. Buster, sensitive by then to his wife's condition, suggested a shopping trip to one of the many outdoor street markets, hoping June would find some bauble he could buy her to effect a reconciliation. On sale were a variety of colourful local wares and foodstuffs. Hats and bangles, dresses and glistening sticky sweets were displayed in disorganized but attractive fashion on the stalls at the back of one of the local beaches.

June failed to respond to Buster's attentions and he was seriously worried that the events of the previous twenty-four hours had significantly damaged their relationship. June walked blindly through the narrow alleyway formed by the stalls, ignoring Buster's frantic attempts to get her interested in an inexpensive but becoming peasant smock. June only had eyes for Nicky as the little girl ran blithely ahead of her parents, causing her mother to haul her back and admonish her more severely than the occasion warranted for running out of her sight.

'Why don't you try this one on, June?' called Buster hopefully, trailing after her with the blouse, to the instant suspicion of the stallholder from whom he had taken it. June swung round to confront him.

'Stop it, Buster. I just don't want it. I didn't even want to come here. It was your idea, this was.'

'All right,' said Buster as reasonably as he could, 'I'll buy it for you. You can take it back if you don't like it.'

'It ain't Marks and Sparks, you know. Nicky!' she yelled loudly, 'Come back here!'

The stallholder and his friend were now convinced that Buster was stealing the smock and prepared to act in concert. It was a normal part of daily life in Acapulco street markets.

'Don't be such a misery guts, June. I'm sorry about what I said at the hospital. Now let's just forget it. It's all over now.'

'No, it ain't, Buster. That's the problem. We don't belong here. This ain't home. It never can be. I gotta go back. I want Mum and I want London and I want the rain and I want Nicky to talk English again!' Her eyes started to fill with tears at the prospect.

'But it's our dream, is this,' said Buster, genuinely puzzled. 'You and me. It's what we both wanted.'

'No, Buster. It ain't *our* dream. It's *yours*. You never asked *me*. All I ever wanted was us. Together. Like we used to be. You remember when we was in hiding together . . .'

'But all that money, the house . . .' interjected Buster, amazed at this outburst.

June looked him squarely in the eye. 'Forget the money, Buster. It's come between us. Can't you see that?'

A cry escaped from Buster's lips that started in the pit of his churning stomach. 'Nooooo, June, please!' He was shattered by her words. It was as if his whole life had been a lie. He simply couldn't believe it. His mind refused to cope with the enormity of what he saw as a betrayal. He made one final attempt to prevent June from walking out on him, but by now the tears had started and were threatening to become a hysterical torrent.

'Leave me, Buster! Leave me alone. Everything's gone now.'

He didn't even think about it. Maybe if he had thought about it he wouldn't have done it. For years he had prided himself on being one of the few men of his acquaintance who never hit his wife. It wasn't a moral rule – he never needed to. He loved June. They had their rows but it ended with a door slamming, not physical abuse. Now he couldn't help it. It was an open palm slap to the face, not a punch, but the effect was the same. June's face coloured, partly out of reaction to the hit, partly out of deep public humiliation. For June the relationship died at that moment. She called Nicky to her, picked her up and ran off with the little girl in her arms. Buster watched her go with an anguish he had never before experienced.

The stallholder made a final attempt to procure payment for the smock Buster still held, incongruously clutched to himself. 'Señor wishes this? I make you good price.'

Buster managed to restrain himself from hitting the man and contented himself with just pushing him away. The stallholder's friend, nevertheless, took exception to this limited aggression and summoned neighbouring stallholders who held Buster down while national revenge was exacted.

CHAPTER EIGHTEEN

Buster decided that it would be quicker to wait for the wounds to close and the bruises to heal of their own accord than to pay a return visit to the hospital. Dragging himself back to the villa slowly and painfully, he tried hard to blank out the prospect of the fight with June that was yet to come. How long would it take before the inevitable reconciliation? The way she had looked at him in the market, it might be a couple of days before life was back on an even keel again.

Ever one of life's optimists, Buster knew that June's current mood was black but she was loyal and she loved him, and that, somehow, excused a great deal. Allowing his mind briefly to touch on the worst possible scenario, he accepted that she might even go and take a holiday for a day or so. His worst fears were realized when he returned to the villa to find the house empty. The trail of possessions he found leading from the bedroom to the front door bothered him and he forgot his physical pain entirely as he made a frantic dash for the hiding place where he kept all their passports. For a second he thought she might have gone to Los Angeles for a day or two. Nicky had so adored Disneyland they had frequently talked about going back to southern California before he remembered that they had all needed visas to cross the frontier into America. She couldn't possibly have obtained an instant visa from the United States embassy. Last time it had taken nearly a week of nervous tension.

*

Fifteen hours later June caught her first sight of England from the steps outside her BOAC 707 as it disgorged its passengers and crew onto the runway at Heathrow Airport. She stood for a moment at the top of the movable stairway, holding the sleeping Nicky in her arms, and smiling as the soft film of drizzle settled invisibly on her face and hair.

Two hours later when the taxi drew up outside Mrs Barker's block of flats, the drizzle had turned to an uncomplicated downpour. June's mood had changed too. The reality of having left Buster started to make her feel unexpectedly depressed. For months she had dreamed of coming home, of stepping out of a black cab, of looking out of the window and seeing the newsagents and the pub and women with heavy overcoats on. Now that the dream had become a reality she couldn't help wondering what Buster was doing, how he had responded to her abrupt departure, what he would do next, how she would get in touch with him without revealing his whereabouts to the police.

Her mother was waiting by the open front door as June and Nicky dashed from the taxi to the flat. Her eyes shone with happiness. June hoped it wasn't triumph, that she wasn't going to spend the next few weeks berating her for having stayed with Buster as long as she had, for having been proved right in the end.

'Please, Mum,' she whispered as she pulled out of the warm embrace, 'Don't say anything. Please.'

Mrs Barker nodded. She understood only too well.

June's return puzzled Jack Mitchell. He sat in the pub with Chalmers, staring long and hard at an inoffensive pint of bitter.

'How do you know he won't be on the next flight?'

'Unlikely,' replied Chalmers shortly. 'He'll know

we'll have spotted his old lady. He's not going to risk getting picked up if we put a twenty-four hour tail on her.'

'No feelers anywhere else?'

'Nothing. If he wanted a deal we'd have heard by now.'

Mitchell drained the glass and replaced it carefully on the beer mat. 'I've lived with those two bastards for nearly three years. Edwards and Reynolds made a monkey out of Dick Poyser. They ain't getting me like that.'

'You don't think it's just a marital tiff do you, sir? And she's run back to her mum.'

Mitchell looked at his detective sergeant witheringly. Is this what all his teaching amounted to?

'No, I sodding well don't,' he said acidly. 'I reckon we'll hear something soon. He's on his way back. I'm sure of it.'

A few months later Buster and Bruce sat among endless cans of beer which they had consumed in the space of a couple of hours, watching the last moments of the World Cup Final between England and West Germany being transmitted live from Wembley Stadium. They had survived the agonies of Germany taking an early lead, Germany equalizing with seconds to go of normal time from a dubious free kick, and the protracted dispute over Geoff Hurst's goal in the first period of extra time when the ball hit the cross-bar and appeared to come down behind the German goalkeeper, although only the Turkish linesman could tell whether or not it had crossed the line. The last five minutes had been pure torture. Surely the Germans couldn't haul themselves off the floor at the death again? The restrained Spanish commentary appeared to the exiled Englishmen disgracefully biased against them.

'Come on, England!' yelled Buster at the set. 'How long left?'

'I make it time,' said Bruce, looking at his watch for the fourth time in the last thirty seconds. 'Blow, you bastard!'

The referee had his whistle in his mouth and the play appeared to stop. He waved his arms for it to continue. A bored Franny drifted in from the bedroom, painting her nails an interesting new shade of violet.

'Nazi twat!' shouted Buster at the black-suited referee.

'I thought you said he was Swiss not a Kraut,' remarked Franny casually. 'That's what you said before.'

The two men sat glued to the screen, entirely oblivious of her presence.

'Is it still two each?' she asked innocently. The men jerked out of oblivion.

'No, it's 3–2, you silly sod,' snapped Bruce irritated. 'Great ball, Bobby Moore,' he called encouragingly, as the English captain hit a superb long ball down the field that appeared to take out almost the entire West German defence. Geoff Hurst fastened onto it as some eager patriots advanced in premature celebration over the touchline. His left-footed shot ripped high into the net beyond the despairing Tilkowski's right hand and the World Cup belonged emphatically to England.

In a squalid drinking den, masquerading as a nightclub in the red-light district of Acapulco, Rosita was entertaining Buster, Bruce and Franny to an evening of celebration in honour of the famous victory. Bruce and Franny found they could adapt with relative ease to most of the social situations in which they found themselves and this was no exception. Buster, on the other hand, had calmed down since the Queen had presented the small gold Jules Rimet trophy to Bobby Moore and was feeling acutely self-conscious about being in a foursome with Rosita and his friends when he wished with all his heart it would have been June standing next to him.

Rosita made no bones about demonstrating overt sexual anticipation. It wasn't for her the prospect of a unique physical experience that made Buster so attractive, but the more practical one that he might be the means of getting her into the much-desired high life of southern California.

The music was loud and the atmosphere hot. Bruce and Franny danced happily together, oblivious of the fact that this wasn't their normal kind of nightclub. The natives were drinking double shots of tequila out of grubby glasses, prompting the speculation from Buster that it was a toss-up which they'd get first – VD or cholera. Bruce and Franny danced easily, cradling cocktail glasses and each other with a grace born of constant practice. Rosita was all over Buster, her hands roving expertly over his body like a cop doing a sensual frisking. She kissed his neck and nibbled his ear, trying to break down his inhibitions. Buster thought he would feel more comfortable breaking and entering a terraced house in Palmers Green.

Bruce and Franny broke off occasionally from their involvement in each other to observe Rosita in full flow. Franny smiled at what she perceived to be Buster's imminent fall from grace, recognizing in Rosita's behaviour the signs of a true artist. Bruce's feelings were a little more ambiguous. He wanted his mate to be happy, of course, but he knew the depth of Buster's love for June. Even if the night's events were to proceed on their appointed course Buster would hate himself in the morning.

It came as no surprise to Bruce to see Buster suddenly wrench himself free of Rosita's cloying embrace. Even through the deafeningly loud music he and Franny heard Buster's agonized 'No!' Buster turned and pushed blindly towards the exit. Franny, concerned, made as if to follow him but Bruce shook his head and restrained her. Buster had to sort this one out himself.

It was barely ten days later when Buster communicated the fateful decision. The two men sat in a living-room that was filthy beyond belief. Plates full of cigarette butts, empty bottles and at least two weeks of dirty dishes lay strewn around the place as Buster and Bruce occupied the only two chairs in the house not piled high with junk of one kind or another. It was an appropriate setting somehow for their recognition that this was the end of the dream.

'You're a fool,' said Bruce in a low voice.

'I'm a fool for not listening before,' replied Buster.

'How d'you know you'll get a deal? You could still go down for thirty.'

'Nah.' Buster had thought about this one a lot and dismissed it. 'Them thirty-year stretches is all over now. Most I'll get is eight or nine. I'll be out in five after remission.'

'Five years in the slammer!' wondered Bruce. 'When you could have all this.' He waved an arm to indicate the distant panorama of sun, sea, sand, surf and sex but all Buster could see was a fortnight's washing up and the likely reaction of his wife if she walked back into that little lot. Without June his life was a wreck in every way.

He tried to explain. 'It don't mean nothing no more, Bruce. Not without her.'

'You're hopeless.' It was an opinion Buster had heard before.

'Wouldn't you do the same if it was Franny?' asked Buster provocatively, knowing the answer in advance. Bruce didn't shake his head but couldn't bring himself to formulate the real answer. Buster's love for June was a very remarkable phenomenon. 'Anyway,' said Buster, suddenly animated, 'I ain't going back to do a deal. I'm going back for June. If I get nicked . . .' Neither of them could finish the sentence and a pall of gloom settled over them again.

Outside a branch of one of the High Street banks in the City of London, a police car, siren wailing, blue light revolving, screeched to a stop. An ambulance and three police cars were already parked haphazardly outside the large Edwardian building and a crowd of interested spectators had been roped away from the scene of the incident. Out of the car stepped Chief Superintendent Mitchell with a face like thunder. Chalmers was waiting for him on the pavement. Together they marched into the building.

In the main hall two ambulance men were calming a hysterical female cashier. Scene-of-crime officers were dusting the tellers' cages looking for fingerprints, but Mitchell and Chalmers were sufficiently involved with other matters to be able to ignore the bank robbery and its aftermath almost entirely.

'I've just been to see the Commissioner, George.'

'And?'

'Bastard won't do it.'

'Shit! Why?'

'Train Robbers still politically sensitive, he says. No deal. I'm really going to get those two now.'

'But we're no damn nearer, sir.'

'If anything,' said Mitchell grimly, 'we're further away. We've reawakened the whole thing and we can't tempt him back with a deal.'

The two men paced the tiled floor in silence while their minds concentrated on the unfairness of life.

'Did the Commissioner realize that if we did a deal we could still have him banged up for eight or nine years? I mean we know his old lady's back here. He's probably on his uppers, wherever he is.'

'Don't talk to me about that silly sod.' Mitchell was still fuming. A uniformed sergeant approached with trepidation.

'Yes, Sergeant?'

'Got 'em, sir. Smashed through the window of an off-licence in Rotherhithe, sir.'

It was a full three seconds before Mitchell grasped that the sergeant was talking about the perpetrators of the bank robbery whom he had supposedly come to arrest.

'Oh,' he said without enthusiasm. 'Great.'

The arrangements had been made, the villa vacated, the Mercedes sold. Buster was in Bruce's apartment dressed in jeans, dark roll-necked jumper and plim-solls preparing to take a last farewell of his friends and of Mexico. The men embraced. 'Don't forget about New Zealand,' Bruce reminded him.

'No. I'll mention it to her.'

'Climate's just like ours,' added Bruce, 'and the food, and she can bring her mum too if she wants.'

'Right,' agreed Buster slightly awkwardly know-ing that the two of them were just going through the motions of planning for the future. Buster's head was just full of thoughts of London and Nicky and, most of all, June.

Franny stepped forward and hugged Buster with genuine warmth and affection.

''Bye, Buster. Give my love to June.'

Buster nodded and picked up the canvas bag that

lay at his feet. He punched Bruce lightly in the stomach.

'I got nearly 400 quid left, you know. Not bad change, I suppose, from 150 grand. You just make sure you don't get caught, right?'

Buster turned on his heel and marched out of Mexico. It was the end of his dream.

It was nearly a week later when a battered old cargo vessel creaked slowly into St Katharine's Dock below Tower Bridge. In the hold Buster was curled up in the foetal position, using his canvas bag as a pillow. A sailor with few delicate sensibilities woke him up by prodding him roughly with the toe of his boot.

'Gerrup, sunshine. We're 'ome.'

Buster groaned and shook himself awake. He started to rise but was forcibly restrained by the sailor's foot. 'How about a small tip?'

Sleepiness and anger fought inside Buster's head for control. 'Piss off,' said Buster with commendable brevity.

'Say 500 quid,' said the sailor, assuming that Buster's response was simply the first round in a complex negotiation.

'Get stuffed,' said Buster as the anger began to dominate the residual sleepiness.

The seaman spat and reached into his pocket. He was going to have to move into the next stage of bargaining more quickly than he had anticipated. He produced a flick knife which had already seen active service. Buster recognized he had limited scope for negotiation now. He sighed. This kind of conversation had been happening to him ever since he had left Leatherslade Farm.

He opened the canvas bag and pretended to scrabble around inside before emerging with an empty fist. 'Sorry. I'm skint.'

The sailor got immediately, and, it seemed to Buster, unreasonably angry. 'You're Buster Edwards. You got bleeding millions. Don't give me none of that crap.'

'There ain't nothing fucking well left,' shouted Buster fed up. 'Look in here, if you don't believe me.'

It was a ploy that had served Buster well in the past and it didn't fail him now. The sailor, as requested, leant forward to look into the bag. It was all Buster needed to knock him off balance. The motion of the cargo boat certainly helped him. The knife clattered to the floor and Buster easily won the perfunctory fight that followed. He scrambled to his feet and prodded the recumbent body of the seaman. He thought about the attempted blackmail and kicked him hard.

'Welcome to Britain,' Buster grinned. He had recovered his sense of humour. The sailor failed to laugh or indeed respond at all for nearly an hour.

Buster moved lightly on his feet, like an athlete, the adrenalin pumping through his veins. He was delighted to be back in England, desperate to hold June and Nicky in his arms again. He slipped down the gangplank and disappeared into the welcoming gloom of St Katharine's Wharf.

Just for the moment Nicky couldn't have been happier. She was 'helping' her grandmother to make a cake by licking the bowl and wooden spoon in which they had mixed the icing. She ignored the doorbell and concentrated exclusively on the difficult final particles of chocolate frosting which were still visible on the mixing bowl. Mrs Barker wiped her hands on her pinny and went into the hall to open the door.

To her enormous surprise she found herself looking

at the smiling face of her son-in-law. Her exclamation was quickly stifled by Buster's hand which was clamped over her mouth as he manoeuvred himself into the flat and shut the front door. 'Hello, Mum. Just popped round for a cuppa tea. All right?' Mrs Barker could only grunt her assent. 'Where are they then?'

Buster slowly removed his hand and allowed her to answer. 'June's upstairs, Nicky's in the kitchen.' Buster moved quickly into the kitchen and picked up his daughter, thinking to himself as he did so how much heavier she had grown in the few months they had been apart.

'Oh, Nicky, I've really missed you,' he gasped as he smothered her with kisses. The little girl squealed with pleasure as he tossed her in the air and tickled her.

'You staying home now, Daddy?' she asked as she recovered from laughing.

'Yes, poppet. Always,' he said fervently.

He nuzzled her again and eventually let her down to the floor. Mrs Barker, for all her general suspicion of Buster and the way in which his selfishness had caused her and her daughter such anguish, couldn't help being touched by the genuine emotion on both sides.

'Nicky, darling,' she began slowly, 'let's get dressed and go to the shops, shall we? We're going to need some more icing sugar 'cause I think we'll have to make another cake now that Daddy's come home.'

Buster smiled his appreciation and put the kettle on. As he poured the hot water into the familiar teapot he felt a warm wave of nostalgia sweep over him for the humdrum pleasures of everyday life in England. Presumably, he thought, this was what June had been feeling all those months in Mexico. He finished his own tea, poured one out for June and mounted the stairs.

In the bedroom which Nicky and June had been sharing, June was making the bed as she heard footsteps on the landing. The polite knock on the door was followed by an enquiry in a bizarre falsetto voice.

'June, darling,' it piped, 'I brought you a cuppa tea.' A thrill of anticipation shot through her. It couldn't be . . . she thought as she strode to the door and flung it open. Standing there was the only love of her life in a pair of navy-blue overalls and with a very silly smile on his face.

Before she could cry out Buster grabbed her in a passionate embrace that was half Hollywood and half for real. The dramatic romantic kiss merged slowly into a full-blown genuine one. Buster paused only to lift June off her feet and toss her onto the bed.

'I just made the bed,' she said irrelevantly.

Buster didn't pause as he continued to tear off his clothes. 'Sometimes,' he observed, 'you say the daftest things.'

Naked, apart from his socks, he hurled himself on her and tried to make up for a lot of lost time.

In fact, what with one thing and another, they didn't leave the room all day. There was, after all, a lot for the two lovers to catch up on. Their bouts of activity were interspersed with long periods of silence when all the eloquence they needed was contained in simply holding one another close. They revelled in the warmth of the physical contact, remembering nearly twenty years of loving and fighting and reconciliation since they had met as teenagers less than two miles from where they now lay.

Even had they known about the telephone call the aching sailor made to Scotland Yard in search of the reward money, they probably still wouldn't have moved. They spoke in low tones of pure contentment.

'Just nothing mattered,' whispered Buster, stroking June's hair and inhaling her scents. 'Not Bruce, not the money, not Mexico.'

'What about that dream?' asked June reasonably.

Buster smiled and let his hands wander deliberately. 'You're my dream, you little sexpot. Ain't never gonna be nobody else.'

When they first heard the sound of a police siren they each stiffened almost instinctively. Then they relaxed. What was done was done and nothing could break the bonds that now united them. Only they could do that to themselves.

'Hey, it's OK,' lied Buster easily. 'I meant to tell you. I done a deal with Mitchell. Me and him, we go way back.'

'Why didn't you tell me?' asked June plaintively.

'Thought you might get cross.'

She snuggled closer to him. She knew perfectly well he was lying. He hadn't made any sort of a deal. He had come back to be with her because he loved her. He was just trying to make his inevitable capture easier for both of them.

'What d'you think you'll get?' asked June as the sound of the siren grew louder and louder.

'Oh, seven or eight,' replied Buster airily. 'I'll be out on parole in four probably. Them thirty-year stretches, they're all finished with.'

The sirens cut out abruptly as the reflection of a revolving blue light shone through the threadbare curtains.

'Will you be waiting?' asked Buster.

''Course I will.'

'Then it don't matter, do it?'

Still naked he hopped out of bed and pulled back the edge of the curtain. Laid out in front of him there appeared to be the entire Metropolitan police force.

The courtyard in front of the block of flats was swarming with police cars, policemen, dogs and dog handlers. Standing by the leading car were Mitchell and Chalmers. Behind them the road was cut off by barriers behind which the police were mounting searchlights in case the arrest turned into a chase across the rooftops.

'Is it the Law?' asked June anxiously from the bed.

Buster surveyed the scene in front of him and let the curtain fall back into place.

'Looks like it,' he replied. 'Shall I make a run for it?'

June shook her head. 'Go and do the deal with Mitchell,' she said after consideration.

'Right,' said Buster, his light voice in contrast to the heaviness of his heart. To have his love returned to him then snatched away again almost in the same instant was more than he could bear.

'I'll be off, then,' he said grinning.

'Ain't you gonna put no trousers on?'

'Thought they might not recognize me like this.'

June laughed out loud. This was the Buster she loved: funny and brave and in love with her. Buster looked longingly at his beautiful wife. He returned to the bed and devoured her with kisses.

June slipped a dressing-gown loosely round her as they came down the stairs together hand in hand. At the foot of the stairs he looked her in the eyes and said pointedly, 'Remember, whatever happens, I love you. It's the only thing that matters.'

He kissed her tenderly for the last time, opened the front door and walked out to face a future in captivity.

The police cars seemed to Buster to be drawn up like a battery of tanks, their headlights shining directly onto the windows of Mrs Barker's tiny flat.

Buster blinked in the glare of the battery of lights and then laughed at the ludicrousness of the whole scene. He stepped forward to meet the waiting policemen.

'Hello, Buster,' said Mitchell, 'Come far, have you?'

'No. I been here for three years, you know. Can't believe you didn't try this place before.'

Chalmers made as if to stem the flow of jokes by brandishing a pair of handcuffs but Mitchell gestured him to put them away. Instead Mitchell opened the rear door of the black Humber Super Snipe and inclined his head ever so slightly like a top people's chauffeur.

Buster grinned at the gesture and turned round to see his wife's little face caught in the narrow opening of the front door. He nodded his head towards Mitchell as if to say, 'See, I'm travelling in style – as usual.' He took a last lingering look at her, that lovely beautiful face, seeking to imprint it on his memory for all time. He smiled broadly and waved at her, that cheeky grin of his etched into his face. As the multitude of police cars roared away, June and Buster both realized at the same time that in the moment of his arrest Buster had managed to turn the whole desperate situation into a personal triumph for him rather than the police who had caught him. They had found a train robber. He had found a kind of glory.

POSTSCRIPT

Buster Edwards stood trial at the Nottinghamshire Assizes on a charge of armed robbery. He was sentenced to fifteen years in prison. He was released on parole after nine years. June was waiting for him. Today he runs a flower stall outside Waterloo Station, just two miles from where they first met in 1947.